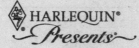

HARLEQUIN®
Presents

What have we got for you in Harlequin Presents books
this month? Some of the most gorgeous men you're
ever likely to meet!

With *His Royal Love-Child,* Lucy Monroe brings
you another installment in her gripping and emotional
trilogy, ROYAL BRIDES; Prince Marcello Scorsolini
has a problem—his mistress is pregnant! Meanwhile,
in Jane Porter's sultry, sexy new story, *The Sheikh's
Disobedient Bride,* Tally is being held captive in
Sheikh Tair's harem...because he intends to tame
her! If it's a Mediterranean tycoon that you're hoping
for, Jacqueline Baird has just the guy for you in *The
Italian's Blackmailed Mistress*: Max Quintano, ruthless
in his pursuit of Sophie, whom he's determined to bed
using every means at his disposal! In Sara Craven's
Wife Against Her Will, Darcy Langton is stunned when
she finds herself engaged to businessman Joel Castille—
traded as part of a business merger! The glamour
continues with *For Revenge...Or Pleasure?*—the latest
title in our popular miniseries FOR LOVE OR MONEY,
written by Trish Morey, truly is romance on the red
carpet! If it's a classic read you're after, try *His Secretary
Mistress* by Chantelle Shaw. She pens her first sensual
and heartwarming story for the Presents line with a
tall, dark and handsome British hero, whose feisty yet
vulnerable secretary tries to keep a secret about her
private life that he won't appreciate.

Check out www.eHarlequin.com for a list of recent
Presents books! Enjoy!

Surrender To The Sheikh

*He's proud, passionate, primal—
dare she surrender to the Sheikh?*

Feel warm winds blowing through your hair
and the hot desert sun on your skin
as you are transported to exotic lands....
As the temperature rises, let yourself be seduced
by our sexy, irresistible sheikhs.

If you love our men of the desert,
look for more stories in this enthralling
miniseries coming soon.

Available only from Harlequin Presents®.

Jane Porter

THE SHEIKH'S DISOBEDIENT BRIDE

Surrender To The Sheikh

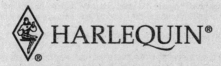

HARLEQUIN®

TORONTO • NEW YORK • LONDON
AMSTERDAM • PARIS • SYDNEY • HAMBURG
STOCKHOLM • ATHENS • TOKYO • MILAN • MADRID
PRAGUE • WARSAW • BUDAPEST • AUCKLAND

ISBN 0-373-12542-9

THE SHEIKH'S DISOBEDIENT BRIDE

First North American Publication 2006.

Copyright © 2006 by Jane Porter.

This edition published by arrangement with Harlequin Books S.A.

® and TM are trademarks of the publisher. Trademarks indicated with ® are registered in the United States Patent and Trademark Office, the Canadian Trade Marks Office and in other countries.

www.eHarlequin.com

Printed in U.S.A.

All about the author...
Jane Porter

Born in Visalia, California, I'm a small-town girl at heart. As a little girl I spent hours on my bed, staring out the window, dreaming of far-off places, fearless knights and happy-ever-after endings. In my imagination I was never the geeky bookworm with the thick Coke-bottle glasses, but a princess, a magical fairy, a Joan-of-Arc crusader.

My parents fed my imagination by taking our family to Europe for a year when I was thirteen. The year away changed me and overseas I discovered a huge and wonderful world with different cultures and customs. I loved everything about Europe, but felt especially passionate about Italy and those gorgeous Italian men (no wonder my very first Presents hero was Italian).

I confess, after that incredible year in Europe, the travel bug bit, and I spent much of my school years abroad, studying in South Africa, Japan and Ireland.

After my years of traveling and studying I had to settle down and earn a living. With my bachelor degree from UCLA in American Studies, a program that combines American literature and American history, I've worked in sales and marketing, as well as a director of a non-profit foundation. Later I earned my master's in writing from the University of San Francisco and taught junior and high school English.

I now live in rugged Seattle, Washington, with my two young sons. I never mind a rainy day, either, because that's when I sit at my desk and write stories about faraway places, fascinating people and, most importantly of all, love.

Jane loves to hear from her readers. You can write to her at P.O. Box 524, Bellevue, WA 98009, USA.

For Lee Hyatt and all readers
who love sheikh stories.

CHAPTER ONE

TALLY heard the guttural shouts seconds before the gunfire. Dropping to her stomach, she hugged her camera and struggled to protect her head.

"Soussi al-Kebir," her guide screamed as he ran from her.

Soussi al-Kebir? Tally pressed her forearm to her face, struggling to make sense of the words with the little Arabic she knew.

Soussi were Berbers from the south, those that lived close to the desert. And al-Kebir was big or great. But *Soussi al-Kebir?*

More gunfire rang in the small town square, the rat-a-tat of machine gunfire and the hard clattering of horses' hooves.

Was this an ambush? Robbery? What?

Heart racing, Tally hugged the cobblestones closer, her camera gripped tightly in the crook of her arm, certain any moment a whizzing bullet would hit her.

Not far from her a man screamed and fell. She heard him hit the ground, the heavy thud of body against stone. Moments later red liquid ran toward her, inches from her face and she recoiled, lifting her head to avoid the blood.

It was then a shadow stretched long above her, the shadow enormous, blocking the intense Barakan sun.

Fear melted Tally's heart. She wanted to squeeze her eyes shut but fear wouldn't let her. She wanted to be brave and bold, but fear wouldn't let her. Instead she huddled there, eyes riveted to the shadow and the foot frighteningly close to her head.

The foot was big and covered in pale suede. The soft leather boot the type desert tribesmen wore, they were made of the softest, most supple leather to protect from the heat of the sand and yet light to make walking in the soft surface easier. White fabric brushed the top of his boot. It was the hem of his robe.

Soussi, she thought, putting it together. The huge shadow. The suede boot. *Soussi al-Kebir.* Chief of the Desert.

Hands encircled Tally's upper arms and she was hauled to her feet. The same hands ripped her camera away from her even as a dark rough fabric jerked down over her head, turning day to night.

Tally screamed as everything went black, but it wasn't the dark fabric that upset her. It was the loss of her camera. Her camera and camera bag were her world, her livelihood, her identity. Without her camera and film, she had no way to pay her bills. No way to survive.

"Give me back my camera!" she demanded, voice muffled by the coarse fabric.

"Quiet!" A harsh male voice commanded.

Suddenly she was lifted, tossed high onto the back of a horse and someone leaped behind her, settling onto the blanket and seizing the reins. Heels kicked at the horse's flanks and they were off, galloping away from the town's medina, down the narrow cobbled street into the desert beyond.

Panicked, Tally struggled in the saddle, battling to pull the fabric off her head but it'd been pulled low and it was tied somehow, anchored around her shoulders.

"Ash bhiti?" She choked in broken Barakan Arabic. *What do you want?*

The only response was an arm pulling her closer, holding her more firmly, the arm thickly muscled, very hard, drawing her against an even thicker, harder torso.

"I have money," she added frantically, growing hotter by the second inside the dark fabric. "I'll give you money. Everything I have. Just go with me to my hotel—"

"Shhal?" he grunted, interrupting her. *How much?*

"Nearly five hundred American dollars."

He said nothing and Tally tried not to squirm even though the fabric was oppressive, suffocating. She had to stay calm, strike a bargain. "I can get more."

"Shhal?" he repeated. He wanted to know how much more she could get.

It was at that point Tally realized she was dealing with a mercenary. "A thousand dollars. Maybe two thousand."

"Not enough," he dismissed, and the arm around her tightened yet again.

"What do you want then?"

"For you to be quiet."

"I—"

"Enough!"

Fear made Tally silent. Fear made her hold her breath, air bottled inside. She'd read about kidnappings in the Middle East. So now instead of fighting further, she told herself not to scream, or thrash. She wouldn't do anything to provoke him, or his men, into doing something that would later be regretted.

Instead she told herself that if she stayed calm, she'd get out of this. If she stayed calm, things might turn out okay.

Not every hostage was punished. Some were released.

That's what she wanted. That's what she'd work to do.

Cooperate. Prove herself trustworthy. Get set free.

To help stay focused, she went over her day, thinking about the way it began, and it began like any other day. She'd loaded her camera with film, put a loose scarf over her head and set out to take her pictures.

She never traveled alone, had learned the value of hiring escorts and guides, bodyguards and translators when necessary. She knew how to slip a few coins into the right hands to get what she wanted.

In remote parts of the world, her native guides and escorts allowed her access to places she normally couldn't visit—temples, mosques, holy cemeteries, inaccessible mountain towns. She'd been warned that being a female would put her in danger, but on the contrary, people were curious and realized quickly she wasn't threatening. Even the most difficult situations she'd encountered were smoothed by slipping a few more coins into a few more hands. It wasn't bribery. It was gratitude. And who couldn't use money?

She'd thought this desert town was no different from the others she'd visited and this morning when she crouched by the medina's well, she'd heard only the bray of donkeys and bleating of goats and sheep. It was market day and the medina was already crowded, shoppers out early to beat the scorching heat.

There'd been no danger. No warning of anything bad to come.

With her camera poised, she'd watched a group of children dart between stalls as veiled women shopped and elderly men smoked. She'd smiled at the antics of the boys, who were tormenting the giggling girls, and she'd just focused her lens when shouts and gunfire filled the square.

Tally wasn't a war correspondent, had never worked for any of the big papers that splashed war all over the front pages, but she'd been in dangerous situations more than once. She knew to duck and cover, and she did the moment she heard the gunfire. Duck and cover was something all children learned on the West Coast in America, earthquakes a distinct possibility for anyone living on one of the myriad of fault lines.

As she lay next to the well, she'd tried to avoid the bright red liquid running between cobblestones and that's when the desert bandit seized her.

If she hadn't looked, maybe the bandit wouldn't have noticed her…

If she hadn't moved maybe she'd be safe in town instead of being dragged into the middle of the desert.

Inside the stifling black fabric Tally struggled to breathe. She was beginning to panic despite her efforts to remain calm. Her heart already beat faster. Air came in shallow gasps.

She could feel it coming on. Her asthma. She was going to have an asthma attack.

Tally coughed, and coughed again.

The dust choked her. She couldn't see, could barely breathe, her throat squeezing closed in protest at the thick clouds of dust and swirling sand kicked up by the wind and the horse's pounding hooves.

Eyes wet with tears, Tally opened her mouth wider, gasping for breath after breath. She was panicking, knew she was panicking and panicking never helped, certainly not her asthma but it was all beyond her, the heat, the jostle of the saddle, the wind, the dust.

Reaching up, out, her hand flailed for contact, grappling with air before landing against the bandit's side. He was warm, hard, too hard, but he was the only one who could help her now. She clung convulsively to the fabric of his robe, tugged on it, hand twisting as frantically as her lungs squeezed.

One, two, she tugged violently on the fabric, her hand twisting in, out, pulling down, against the body, anything to express her panic, her desperation.

Can't breathe…

Can't breathe…

Can't…

Tair felt the hand grappling with his shirt, felt the wild frantic motion and then felt her go slack, hand falling away limply.

He whistled to his men even as he reined his horse, drawing to a dramatic pawing stop.

Tair threw the fabric covering off the foreign woman captured in the town square.

She was limp and nearly blue.

He lifted her up in one arm, turned her cheek toward him, listened for air and heard nothing.

Had he killed her?

Tipping her head back, he covered her mouth with his own, pinched her nose closed, blowing air into her lungs, forcing warm air where there had been none.

His men circled him on their horses forming a protective barrier, although they should be safe here. This was his land. His people. His home. But things happened. They knew. He knew.

He felt their silence now, the stillness, the awareness. They wouldn't judge him, they wouldn't dream of it. He was their lord, their leader, but no one wanted a death on his hands. Especially not a foreign woman.

Much less a young foreign woman.

Not when Ouaha still fought for full independence. Not when politics and power hung in delicate balance.

He covered her mouth again, forcing air through her once more, narrowed gaze fixed on her chest, watching her small rib cage rise. Come on, he silently willed, come on, Woman, breathe.

Breathe.

And he forced another breath into her, and another silent command. You will breathe. You will live.

You will.

She sputtered. Coughed. Her lashes fluttered, lifted, eyes opening.

Grimly Tair stared down into her face, the pallor giving way to the slightest hint of pink.

Alhumdulillah, he silently muttered. Thanks be to God. He might not be a good man, or a nice man, but he didn't enjoy killing women.

Her eyes were the palest brown-green, not one color or the other and although her expression was cloudy, unfocused, the color itself was remarkable, the color of a forest glen at dawn, the forest he once knew as a boy when visiting his mother's people in England.

Her brows suddenly pulled, her entire face tightening, constricting. She wheezed. And wheezed again, lips pursing, eyes fixed on him, widening, eyes filled with alarm.

Her hand lifted, touched her mouth, fingers curving as if to make a shape. Again she put her hand to her mouth, fingers squeezing. "Haler."

He shook his head, impatient, not understanding, seeing the pink in her skin fade, the pallor return. She wasn't getting air. She wasn't breathing again.

Her eyes, wide, frightened, held his and her fear cut him. She was hurt and in pain and he was doing this to her.

"What do you need?" he demanded, switching to English even as he lightly slapped her cheek, trying to get her to focus, communicate. What was wrong? Why couldn't she breathe?

Her fingers merely curled, reminding him of the letter C from the Western alphabet as she gasped, and he blocked out her frantic gasps of air studying fingers instead. And then suddenly he knew. Asthma.

"You have asthma," he said. He was gratified to see her nod. "Where is your inhaler?"

"Cam-ra."

He lifted a hand, gestured, signaling he wanted it. The bag was handed over immediately.

Tair unzipped the top, rifled through, found the inhaler in a small interior side pocket and shook it before putting it to her mouth. Her hand reached up, released the aerosol, letting it flood her lungs.

Still holding her in the crook of his arm he watched her take another hit, saw her chest rise and fall more slowly, naturally, saw that she was breathing more deeply and he felt a measure of relief. She lived. He hadn't killed her. Good.

Hard to explain a dead Western woman to the authorities.

Minutes later she stirred again.

Tally didn't know at exactly what moment she realized she was lying in the barbarian's arms, her legs over his, her body in his lap, but once she knew where she was, and how he held her, she jerked upright.

She wrenched free, attempted to jump from the horse but instead fell to the ground, tumbling in a heap at everyone's feet.

She groaned inwardly, thinking she was getting too old for dramatic leaps and falls. Tally rose, straightening her white cotton shirt and brushing her khaki trousers smooth. "Who are you?" she demanded.

The man on the horse adjusted his headcovering, shifting the dark fabric to conceal all of his face but his eyes and bridge of nose. Face covered, he just looked at her, as did the others, and there were about a half dozen of them altogether.

"What do you want with me?" she persisted.

"We will talk later."

"I want to talk now."

He shrugged. "You can talk but I will not answer."

Tally inhaled, felt the hot still air slide into her lungs. She couldn't believe this was happening. It made no sense. Nothing about this made sense. She'd been kidnapped from the medina, taken right from the market by a group of masked men. But why?

Who were they?

Her gaze settled on the soft suede boot in front of her, the color light, cream, just slightly darker than the white robe. Her gaze rose, lifting from the pale suede boot which covered from foot to calf, up over his knee, to the horse's ornate saddle and bridle. Both were made from pounded silver, heavily decorated with bits of onyx and blue stone, finished with colorful woolen tassels. The bridle's decorative leather curved protectively around the neck, nearly covered the ears, shielding the eyes. More silver and leatherwork ran across the front of the horse to match the saddle.

Tally's gaze lifted higher, moving from horse to man. He, in comparison, was dressed simply. White pants and robe, and a dark headcloth that wrapped around the neck, covered the head, and cloaked his face from nose to throat.

His eyes she could see. And they were dark, fixed, penetrating, nearly as strong as the bridge of his nose.

"Who are you?" she asked.

"We will talk later," he said, and turning slightly in his silver and gold embroidered blanket that served as a saddle, gestured to his men. "We go."

"No."

"No?"

"You nearly killed me!" Her voice was deep, raspier than usual.

He shrugged. "Fortunately I also saved you."

"And you what? Expect thanks?"

"Indeed. If it weren't for me, you would have died."

"If it weren't for you, I'd still be in town. Safe."

"It's a moot point. You're here now." He shifted on the embroidered blanket, reins loose in his palm as his gaze swept the barren landscape. "And this is where you want to stay? In the middle of the desert, on your own?"

Tally glanced right, left, saw only sand and pale dunes, the world a stunning ivory and gold vista in every direction. "We're just hours from the nearest town."

"Hours by horse." His head cocked and he studied her curiously, black eyebrows flat above intense eyes. "Do you have a horse?"

She felt her spine stiffen, her teeth clamping tight in the back of her jaw. "Not unless you kidnapped one for me."

"I'm afraid I did not."

"Right. Well, then, no horse."

He leaned down, out of his saddle so that his face loomed above hers. "I guess you'll be coming with me." And before she could protest, he swept her into his arm and deposited her on the saddle in front of him, back onto his lap from where she'd only just escaped.

Tally grunted as she dropped onto his lap. Damn. His lap was big, hard, just like the rest of him. Soussi al-Kebir. Chief of the Desert, indeed. "What group are you part of?" she asked, unable to remain silent despite her best intentions. She needed to know the worst.

"Group?" her captor grunted, even as he resettled her more firmly into his lap, his left arm slung around her, holding her against his hips.

She squirmed inwardly at the contact. "Who are you with?"

"With?"

If ever there was a time to be sensitive—diplomatic— this was it. But it wasn't easy finding the right words, or the right tone. "You must be part of a group, a tribe maybe?"

She felt him exhale. "You talk too much," he said exasperatedly even as he urged his horse into a canter. "Practice silence."

They rode the rest of the day in virtual silence, traveling deep into the desert, racing across the sand for what seemed like hours. Tally had given up sneaking glances at her watch. Time no longer mattered. They weren't close to anybody or anyplace that could help her. There was no one here to intercede on her behalf. The only thing she could do was stay alert, try to keep her wits about her, see if she couldn't find a way out.

Just before twilight they slowed, horses trotting as they reached the bandits' camp city, an oasis of tents and camels in what seemed to be the middle of nowhere.

At the camp, the men dismounted quickly. Tally's bandit jumped from his horse but when he reached for her, Tally squirmed away and dismounted without his help. She'd had enough of his company and wanted nothing more to do with him. But of course her captor had other plans for her.

"Come," he said, snapping his fingers. "Follow me."

He led her past a group of men sitting on the ground, and then past another group of men cleaning guns. She gave the second group of men a long, hard look. Guns were not good. This situation was not good.

Her bandit stopped walking, gestured to a tent on his left. "You'll go there," he said.

She looked at the tent and then the tribesman. "It's a tent."

"Of course it's a tent," he answered impatiently. "This is where we live."

She looked back to the tent, the fear returning, squeezing her insides, making it hard to breathe. "Is this a temporary stopping point?"

"Temporary, how? What are you asking?"

"Are we traveling on tomorrow?"

"No."

"Then what are we doing here?"

"Stopping." He gestured to the tent. "Go inside. Dinner will be brought to you."

Tally faced the tattered goatskin tent. It was hideous. Stained, patched, and worn. She'd been traveling in Northern Africa and the Middle East for six months now and she'd never seen such a rough encampment before. This was not a friendly camp. This was not a nomadic tribe, either. There were no children here, no women, no elderly people. Just men, and they were heavily armed.

Tally didn't know who they were and she wasn't sure she wanted to find out, either. Survival was paramount in her mind at this point.

She turned to look at her captor. He was tall, and hard and very indifferent. She suppressed a wave of emotion. No tears, no distress, no sign of weakness, she reminded herself. "How long will you keep me here?"

"How long will you stay alive?"

A lump filled her throat and she bit her lip, hot, exhausted, grimy. "Do you intend to…kill…me?"

His dark eyes narrowed, and a muscle pulled in his jaw, tightening the weathered skin across his prominent cheekbones. He had a strong nose, broad forehead and no sympathy or tenderness in his expression. "Do you *want* to die?"

What a question! "No."

"Then go inside the tent."

But she didn't move. She couldn't. She'd stiffened, her limbs weighted with a curious mixture of fear and dread. While she hated how he snapped his fingers as he ordered her about, it was the cold shivery dread feeling in her belly that made her feel worse.

She hated the dread because it made her feel as if nothing would ever be okay again.

"What do I call you?" she asked, nearly choking on her tongue, a tongue that now felt heavy and numb in her mouth. Tally had been in many dangerous situations but this was by far the worst.

He stared down at her for a long, tense moment. As the silence stretched, Tally looked past him, spotted a group of bearded men still meticulously cleaning their guns.

"Do you have a name?" Her voice sounded faint between them.

"Seeing as you're from the West, you can call me Tair."

"Tair?" she repeated puzzled.

He saw her brow crease with bewilderment but didn't bother to explain his name, seeing no point in telling her that his real name was something altogether different, that he'd been born Zein el-Tayer, and that he was the firstborn of his father's three sons and the only son still alive. He'd survived the border wars and the past ten years of tensions and skirmishes due to a lethal combination of skill and luck.

In Arabic, Zein or Zain meant "good", but no one called him Zein even if it was his first name because he wasn't good. Everyone in Baraka and Ouaha knew who he was, what he was, and that was danger. Destruction.

Tair wasn't a good man, would never be a good man and maybe that was all his captive needed to know.

"You'll be fine if you do what you're told," he added shortly, thinking he'd already spent far more time conversing than he liked. Talking irked him, it wasted time. Too many words filled the air, cluttering space, confusing the mind. Far better to act. Far better to do what needed to be done.

Like he'd done today.

He'd removed the threat from town, away from his people. He'd keep the woman isolated, too, until he understood what she was doing in his land, and who—or what—had brought her here in the first place.

Single women—and single women with cameras—didn't just happen upon Ouaha. If Western women visited Ouaha, which didn't happen very often, they were part of a tour, something that had been organized by a trusted source, and their itinerary was publicized, known.

"How did you get to Ouaha?" he asked abruptly, studying her wan face. She looked tired, but there was nothing defeatist in her expression. Rather she looked fierce. Furious. A wild animal cornered.

"Airplane to Atiq, and then jeep and camel from there."

"But someone planned your itinerary."

"I planned it myself. Why?"

The flare of heat in her eyes matched the defiant note in her voice. If she was afraid or worried, she gave no outward appearance. No, she looked ready for battle and that fascinated him. But it wasn't just her expression that intrigued him. It was her face. Strong through the brow, cheekbone and jaw, and yet surprisingly soft at the mouth with full, rose pink lips. Her gaze was direct, focused, not at all shy.

She had the look of a woman who knew her mind, a woman who wasn't easily influenced or deceived, which made him wonder about her appearance in Ouaha.

"I'm the one to ask the questions. You're the one to answer.

Go now to your tent. I shall speak with you later." Tair turned and walked away, but not before he saw her jaw drop and the blaze of fury in her eyes.

This woman didn't like being told what to do. His lips curved as he returned to his men. She'd learn soon to mask her true feelings or she'd simply continue playing into his hand.

CHAPTER TWO

TALLY watched the bandit—Tair, he'd said his name was—walk away. She noticed he hadn't even waited for her to respond. He'd ordered her in and then just walked away knowing she had no choice but to obey.

She clutched the tent flap, and stared at his retreating back, watching his white robe flow behind him.

Tally swore silently. Think, she told herself, do something. *But what?*

She caught the eye of one of the men cleaning guns and his expression was so disapproving that Tally shivered, and swiftly stepped into the tent.

But once inside, Tally didn't know what she was supposed to do. The tent was crude. There were few furnishings—just a low futonlike bed, a blanket of sorts, a small chest and a couple of pillows on the bed—and nothing remotely decorative. No wardrobe for clothes (not that she had any!), no chair, no mirror, nothing.

It would have been so easy to panic, but Tally resisted falling apart. There was little point in giving way to hysterics. No one even knew she was gone. No one would know she was missing. As far as her family knew, she'd been missing for years.

Sighing, she rubbed her brow, feeling the grit of sand and dust at her temple, against her scalp. Riding across the desert had been an illuminating experience. She could have sworn she ate more sand and dust than what they'd traveled over thanks to the horses' flying hooves.

Loosening her ponytail, Tally pulled the elastic from her hair and dragged her fingers through her hair, working the kinks free. What was going to happen now?

What was she supposed to do? Run? Steal a horse? Make vague threats about human rights and government relations?

Lifting the weight of her hair from her neck, she let her nape cool. She felt hot and sticky all over. Hot, sticky and afraid.

Why was she here? Were they going to ransom her? Punish her? What?

What did they want with her?

Reluctantly Tally pictured Tair, the bandit who'd taken her from town, and her stomach did a dramatic free fall all the way to her toes. Tair wasn't like the others. He was bigger, harder, fiercer. The way he'd held her as they rode today had been possessive, the very way his arm curved around her, his hand against her stomach sent shockwaves of alarm through her. It was as if he'd laid claim to her, a statement of ownership.

But she wasn't his. She'd never be his.

Her stomach did another nosedive and goose bumps covered her arms. Irritably she rubbed at her arms, trying to ignore the crazy adrenaline ricocheting through her.

He hadn't let her die in the desert. When she'd had her asthma attack he'd forced air into her lungs and then found her inhaler. He obviously didn't want her dead. But then what did he want from her? And would anyone back in Seattle care if she never returned?

Don't be a pessimist, she rebuked herself severely. *You're a freelance photographer, and maybe you've never deliberately photographed war, but you knew that life in the desert wasn't without violence.*

For a moment Tally felt calmer, stronger, at least she did until her tent flap snapped open and a dark shadow filled the opening.

Tally's stomach jumped, her heart plummeted. God help her. The bandit was back.

Dropping her hair, she smoothed her white cotton shirt over the waistband of her khaki slacks and watched as he entered her tent. He had to stoop to get through the covered opening. Once inside he glanced casually around, as if taking stock.

Tally swallowed hard, hands knotted at her sides. "Can you tell me why I'm here?" she asked, trying to sound conversational, not confrontational.

The tent flap swished behind him, allowing in bits of the twilight. He'd changed, and his outer robe hung open over a loose shirt and fitted pants. "You've interesting friends," he said, after a long tense pause.

"I don't understand. What friends are you talking about?"

"The friends you've been traveling with."

Her forehead furrowed. "I'm on my own. I've traveled with no one."

"You had men with you this morning."

"Ah." Her expression cleared. Comprehension, as well as relief swept over her. "Those men worked for me. They're Barakan. One was my translator. The other a guide."

He said nothing so she pushed on, praying she sounded confident, reasonable. "I hired them in Atiq and they knew I wanted to visit the kasbahs on the other side of the Atlas Mountains."

"How much did they pay you?"

Tally felt a prickle behind her eyes, pain that reminded her of the migraines she used to get when she was in college. "They didn't pay me. I paid them. As I said, I hired them. Their names were given to me by the hotel and they came highly recommended."

"And did they do what you wanted?"

"Yes. Until this morning there'd been no problem."

He regarded her for a long silent moment. "Why did you want to come to Ouaha?"

"Is that where I am?"

"Don't act so surprised."

"I am surprised. I hadn't realized we'd left Baraka. There was no border crossing—"

"A desert separates the countries, Woman."

She flinched at the "woman" but didn't contradict him. Instead she took a breath, suppressing her aggravation. "There was no plan to come to Ouaha. I merely told my guides what I wanted and they set the course knowing I needed to be in Casablanca by the first of October."

"Why the first of October?"

"My visa for Baraka ends and I need to be in Morocco by then."

His thickly fringed eyes narrowed, his angular jaw thickening yet again. "And so what exactly are you doing here, so far from your home?" His voice had dropped, and it was low, low and deadly.

"Nothing. Just sightseeing."

"With rebels as your guides?"

Her pulse quickened yet again. She pressed her palms together, the skin damp, sticky. "I don't know their politics. We never discussed—"

"But you paid them."

"Yes. I needed them. This part of the world is remote, and often inaccessible for women. I needed experienced guides."

"You're sure they didn't pay you?"

Tally would have laughed if the situation weren't so precarious. "For what?"

He slowly crouched down in front of the bed until he was eye to eye with her. His dark gaze met hers, held, the set of his mouth anything but gentle. "Why don't you tell me."

His eyes were so dark, and the expression so intense that Tally felt her heart stutter, not just with fear, but awareness. She knew men and was comfortable with men but Tair wasn't like men she'd ever known. There was an untamed element to him, a primitive maleness that made her feel increasingly small, fragile, female. And she didn't like feeling small or fragile, she just wasn't. Life had toughened her. She didn't frighten easily.

Swallowing, Tally gathered her courage. "I have no idea what you want from me. I'm just a tourist—"

"Not just a tourist. You've spent two weeks with those men. Two weeks photographing, documenting." His voice dropped even lower, deeper, and the husky ominous pitch slid down Tally's spine.

"We'll try this one more time," he said slowly, quietly, "and I warn you, I'm not a patient man but I'm trying. So don't test me. Understand?"

She nodded, because she did understand, and she also understood that things weren't going well and if they didn't come to some kind of agreement relatively soon, she would be in even greater danger. "Yes."

"Now tell me about the men you were traveling with."

"I know very little about them. They were quiet. They kept to themselves quite a bit. I thought they were good men."

"You've been with them two weeks and this is all you can tell me?"

How did he know she'd been traveling for two weeks with the men? He'd either been told, or he'd been watching her. Either way she'd been followed. "I'm sorry," she said, picking her words with care. If ever there was a time for diplomacy, this was it. "We didn't speak much. They're men. I was a foreign woman. There were cultural differences."

"Cultural differences."

She flushed, locked her fingers together. "I wish I could tell you more. I hadn't thought I was doing anything wrong. I've always wanted to visit Baraka—"

"But you're not in Baraka anymore. This is Ouaha. An independent territory, and this is my country, and these are my people and you entered my country with Barakan rebels. Men who have brought violence and destruction to my people."

She shook her head. "I don't know what you're talking about. I arrived in Atiq, hired these men as escorts, and yes, I have been traveling with them but that's because I'm a tourist, and traveling alone. I needed local guides and they came highly recommended."

"What about your pictures?" he asked, eyes narrowing.

She paled. "What about them?"

"You were taking pictures for them, weren't you?"

"No. They were for me. I didn't work for those men. Those men worked for me. The pictures are for me."

"Why do you want photographs of a nation so far from your own?"

For a moment Tally didn't know how to answer. His question had rendered her speechless. Why would she be interested in something so far from her home? Had he no desire to see the world, know something of places foreign to him? Finally she found her voice. "Because I'm curious."

"Curious about what?"

"Everything. Food, culture, language, lifestyle. I'm fascinated by people, by the differences among us, as well as what we have in common, too."

He snorted, a deep, rough sound of contempt. "We've nothing in common."

She couldn't hide her own flash of disdain, her jaw tightening, temper flaring. This is one of the reasons she traveled, as well as one of the reasons she'd left home. She'd abhorred ignorance and control. "Perhaps not. But instead of me staying home and sitting in my living room twiddling my thumbs, I've decided to go out and discover the truth for myself."

"Women belong at home."

"Maybe in your opinion—"

"Yes. In my culture women have a vital role taking care of

the children, watching over the family, making sure her husband is fed and rested. Comfortable."

"And when does she get to be fed and rested? When is she comfortable?"

"She is comfortable when her family is healthy and at peace."

"Huh!" Tally scoffed scornfully. "Why do I get the feeling that never happens?"

He swore something in Arabic she couldn't catch but from his tone she knew it wasn't kind. She'd angered him. She felt his hostility rolling off him in waves. She also felt his ambivalence. He couldn't decided what to do with her and Tally bit her lip, knowing she'd pushed him too hard, said too much. She'd never been a big talker but she'd certainly said quite a bit since arriving here.

"I'm sorry," she said, struggling to be conciliatory. "I'm just a curious person by nature, and I'm here in Baraka—"

"Ouaha."

"Ouaha," she amended, not really knowing anything about the territory but anxious to move on, "because I'm curious about your part of the world. I don't want to be ignorant."

"So you're just a tourist."

He was testing her, she thought, probing for the truth and her insides knotted, twisting with apprehension. No, she wasn't just a tourist. She was a professional photographer but right now she didn't think that would go over real well. He already mistrusted her. Would his opinion change when she told him she was in his country taking pictures for a book on children? "Yes, a tourist," she echoed.

"And that's the truth?"

She regarded him steadily even as she scrambled to consider all the angles. It wasn't a complete lie. She was a tourist, and she did love travel and discovering faraway places. Why did he have to know about her work? Why couldn't she just be a traveler with a camera?

Tally held his gaze. "Yes," she said, proud that her voice didn't wobble in the slightest.

"We'll see, won't we?" he answered even as a voice sounded from outside the tent.

Her bandit shouted back and the tent flap suddenly lifted and a man entered carrying her camera. The man handed her camera to Tair and then left without once ever looking at her.

As the bandit handled her camera, pulling it from the leather case and turning it over, Tally's legs went weak. She had a sudden desire to sit. But she didn't dare move and instead she watched as he pushed buttons, turned the camera on and off, zoomed the telephoto lens out before bringing it back.

It made her nervous, watching him play with her camera. It was a good camera but not the most expensive on the market. However the pictures were important and the memory disk was full. She'd planned on putting in a new disk today, after she left the market.

"Tell me what you're looking for," she said now, careful to keep her voice calm, "and I'll show you."

He ignored her. Instead he opened the cover and then slid open the memory card slot. She watched as he tapped the small blue memory card, popping it out. Tally dug her nails into her hands. The card was tiny, looked like nothing, and yet it was everything to her. Her work, her life, her future.

"That's more or less the film," she said. "It's a digital camera which means it uses a memory card instead of 35 millimeter film."

He held the blue card up, twisting it one way and then the other.

Her heart was in her throat. It was as if he held her whole life in his hands. "I know it's very small, but it holds hundreds of photos."

"Are there hundreds of photos here?"

Reluctantly she nodded.

"Do you have other cards?" he asked.

Tally chewed on the inside of her cheek. She didn't want to tell him that she had months of work on the memory cards, hundreds and hundreds of photos she hadn't managed to download to her editors in New York or save to CD-ROM yet. Everything she'd done since April was on the memory cards in the camera bag and her hotel room. "Yes."

"Where are they?"

Oh God. He wasn't going to take them from her, was he? He wasn't going to destroy her work? "Why?"

He shrugged. "They're just pictures. You don't need them. It's not why you're here. You're a tourist. You're here for the experience, not photographs."

She exhaled so hard and sharp it hurt. Her eyes burned. She fought to remain calm. "But the photos are important. They help me remember where I've been and what I've seen."

"You seem anxious," he said, slipping the memory card back into the camera and clicking the card-slot door closed.

She was anxious. She was trembling. "Can I please have my camera back?"

"Maybe. When I'm finished. But you'll get it back without the memory card."

"The camera won't work without it."

"You can always buy new ones."

"But I'll lose everything I've done."

"They sell postcards in town. Buy those on your way home." He turned to leave but she rushed toward him.

"Please," she cried, stopping herself from touching him, knowing instinctively that that would be bad. She was already in trouble. She couldn't risk offending him more than she already had. "Please don't erase my photos. I'll show them to you. I'll explain the camera to you—"

"I haven't time," he interrupted turning to walk away. "Dinner will be brought to you soon. I'll see you tomorrow."

"Tomorrow." Tally's heart raced, fueled by fear and fury. It was a maddening combination and her hands shook from the adrenaline of it. "You're going to leave me here until tomorrow? And then what happens? Will you give me my camera back then, and the film?"

"Dinner will be brought soon," he repeated tonelessly.

But Tally wouldn't simply be dismissed. She didn't understand what any of this was about. She'd paid her guides good money and yet when the shots rang out in the medina this morning, the men had just left her. They ran. Well, both ran. One was shot. She shivered in remembrance. "What is it that you want with me?"

"We'll talk after I've gone through your pictures."

"You won't delete anything, will you?"

"It depends."

"On *what?*"

"What I find." His dark head nodded. "Good night."

Tally threw herself on her low bed, buried her face in the pillow and howled with rage. He could not do this! He could not!

She couldn't accept it. Wouldn't. What he did was wrong, and unjust.

In his tent, Tair slouched low in his chair, closed his eyes, doing his best to shut out the American woman ranting in the tent not far from his.

She needed to accept her fate more gracefully. Surrender with dignity. He was almost tempted to tell her so, too, but she might perceive it as some hard won victory and he wouldn't get her the satisfaction.

First she'd yield.

Then he'd show mercy.

Not the other way around.

Besides, his father had kidnapped his wife—Tair's own mother—and his father was a good man. Decent. Fair. Well, fair enough.

Eventually the American woman would realize that Tair was just as decent, if not fair.

* * *

Tally ended up crying herself to sleep. She didn't remember falling asleep, just weeping and punching her pillow. But now it was morning and opening her eyes, she stretched.

Her eyes still burned from the tears and it took a moment for her to focus. Tiredly her gaze settled on the small chest at the side of the bed. Oh God. She was still here. The tent. The encampment. Tair's world.

It wasn't just a bad dream. It was a bad reality.

Groaning Tally stretched an arm down, reached for the pillow that had fallen from her bed and bunched it under her cheek.

Okay. Last night she'd fallen apart. Today was strategy. Today she'd get her camera and film back. It was hers, after all, not his.

Already dressed in her thin cotton khaki slacks and white shirt, Tally left her tent in search of answers. Like who the hell was in charge of Ouaha.

Stalking out of her tent, she felt the intense desert sun pour over her, blinding her, scorching her almost immediately from head to toe. It was hot. A blistering heat, a heat unlike anything she'd ever known, either, and she'd been in some hot places before. The Brazilian jungle. The Outback in January. Marfa, Texas in July.

"Lady!" An elderly Berber man rushed toward her. He was thin, slight and stooped but he moved quickly. "Lady!" he repeated urgently, gesturing to the tent flap.

Tally felt the corner of her mouth lift in a faint, dry smile. She was supposed to go back inside the tent, sit and wait like a good little girl, wasn't she?

The corner of her mouth lifted in an even drier smile. Too bad she wasn't a good little girl anymore.

The old Berber turned and ran, and Tally suspected he'd gone in search of Tair. Good. She wanted to see him.

But as Tally passed one tent, she spotted on a chest outside another tent a leather case that looked suspiciously like her camera bag. Tally glanced around, no one was near by, everyone busy with tasks elsewhere and took several steps closer.

It was her camera bag and it was partially unzipped. She could see her camera tucked inside.

Tally sucked in a breath. The camera was so damn close. She had to get it back. At the very least, she had to get the memory card out before the bandit destroyed any photos.

Crouching down next to the chest, Tally pulled her camera from the bag, opened the card slot, popped the memory card out, closed the slot, dropped the camera back into the bag and stood up to return to her tent.

But suddenly the old Berber was in front of her, a long cotton gown draped over his arm.

Tally didn't know what he was saying but once he unfurled the robe she knew he wanted her to cover up.

"No, thank you," she said, shaking her head. "I'm fine. I'm just going back to my tent now anyway."

But he insisted and the more he insisted the faster Tally tried to walk, but he wouldn't stop talking and he was drawing attention to them.

Cheeks burning, Tally finally took the robe and tugged it over her head. "Thank you," she said stiffly. "Now if I can just go back to my tent?"

But the old man was still talking and gesticulating and Tally clutched the small memory card tighter, her palm beginning to grow damp. She had to get the card hidden before Tair appeared.

Finally she managed to escape, slipping beneath the flap of her tent and diving onto her bed. She was shaking all over. Shaking with fear, shaking with relief. But she had the memory card back. That was the important thing.

But where to hide it? She still hadn't decided when she heard voices outside her tent. She was out of time. Hastily Tally tucked the memory card under her shirt, inside her bra just as the tent flap flipped over and Tair's long shadow stretched over the floor, his powerful frame silhouetted by the bright morning sun.

"You lied to me and you stole from me," his deep voice rasped. "If you were a man I'd cut your tongue out and you'd lose a hand."

Tally wrapped her arms around her knees, hugging them for protection.

"Where is the memory card?" he demanded.

Tally hugged her knees even tighter. "What are you talking about?"

"You know perfectly well."

"I don't."

He said nothing now, just stared at her, his expression hard, unforgiving, brooding. His eyes were dark like coffee and a deep line seemed permanently etched between his black eyebrows.

He finally spoke. "I saw you. I was watching."

Tally shuddered. She felt his anger and scorn, it was also there in his eyes and the mocking tilt of his lips but she wouldn't let him know it bothered her. And she wouldn't act afraid, or acknowledge that she was stuck here. Stranded and powerless.

"I want it," he added softly. "Now."

"It's mine!" she answered fiercely, even as she bowed her head. She couldn't give him the memory card, she couldn't. It was hers, all she had of the past few weeks.

"Before you tell me no again," he added even more quietly, "before you tell me another lie, know that in my world thieves lose hands. Liars lose tongues. Think for a moment. Decide if your photos are worth it."

Tally couldn't look at him now. All thoughts of being tough and strong were crumbling. "Please," she whispered. "Please let me keep the card. You can have the camera."

"That's an odd thing for a tourist to say."

Slowly Tally lifted her head, swallowing around the lump of fear.

"You told me you were just a tourist," he added, his dark eyes boring into her, staring so hard, so intently she felt as if he were seeing inside her, all the way to her heart. "You lie. You steal. What else do you do?"

She shook her head, terrified.

"Perhaps you aid the insurgents. Those who want to be rid of us. Those that take our land from us."

"I help no one—"

"Why should I believe you?"

"Because I'm not political. Yes, I'm a photographer, but I'm not political, I take no sides, I do not even know the history of these border wars you talk about."

"Prove it."

She looked at him for a long unblinking moment. "How?"

"Give me the memory card back. I will look at the photos. I shall see for myself if you tell the truth."

She couldn't look away from his dark eyes, or his hard features, each strong, defined—nose, jaw, cheekbone, brow bone. "What if you don't like my work?"

He shrugged. "I'll erase it."

Tears filled her eyes and she hated herself for being weak and emotional but she was in agony. Those photos were months of work, work in nearly unbearable heat, work in wretched conditions, work where she'd sacrificed comfort and her own health to get just the right shots. "Please don't erase my work. I've weeks and weeks of shots on that memory card. I haven't downloaded anything in ages since I've been traveling."

He was still, very still and his hard gaze reproving. "Why did you lie to me?"

She searched his face, searched for a sign of compassion or comprehension. "I didn't think you'd understand."

He stared down at her, expression shuttered, and when he spoke his voice was cold. "No. I don't understand." Then he walked out and for a moment Tally did nothing and then leaping from the bed, she chased after him.

"Wait," she shouted, running to catch up with him. "Wait, please. Please!" She caught his sleeve, tugged on it. Her legs were shaking, her heart pounding and her mouth tasted sandy and dry.

Reaching into her bra, Tally pulled out the memory card and with a trembling hand gave it to him. "Take it. Look at the photos. See what I've done, see my work for yourself. If certain pictures offend you, then erase those, but I beg you, please don't delete everything. Please leave me something." Her voice cracked, broke. "I've spent months here, months in the desert, months away from my family. Please don't take it all from me."

Silently he accepted the memory card, his large hand wrapping around the small disk. Tally met his gaze, and blinking back tears she held it, looked him square in the eye, looked without pretense or pride. She was asking him to be fair, that's all she wanted. For him to be fair.

Legs still shaking, she walked back to her tent, and dropped weakly onto the low bed.

This wasn't good. So not good.

This is exactly what her mother always warned her about. This was what her friends had predicted. This was what her editor cautioned every time Tally set out on a new expedition. But she'd been a photographer for years and although she'd been in some tight spots, she'd never had serious trouble. She'd been doing so well traveling on her own until now. But this…this…was bad.

CHAPTER THREE

TALLY wasn't alone long. Almost immediately her captor returned with her camera and bag. He dropped them on to the bed next to her and she grabbed them, held the camera and case to her as though they were her last lifeline to the outer world.

"Why?" she stammered, looking up at him.

He shrugged. "You said the camera wouldn't work without the memory card."

For a moment she didn't see where he was going with this, and then she understood. Even as she searched her camera bag she knew all the memory cards were gone. He'd kept them. Her pleasure in having the camera returned dimmed. "I shouldn't have given you it back," she said bitterly. "I should have protected my pictures."

"It didn't matter if you gave it back to me or not. The card you took from the camera was blank. It was a new memory card. I switched the cards before I left the camera out."

Tally shoved a hand through her hair, pushing it off her face. She was so hot she wanted to scream. Throw things. Pick a fight. "You didn't. You're bluffing."

"Bluffing?" His gaze locked with hers. "Is that what I think you just said."

Her heart pounding, she held his gaze, showing him once and for all she wouldn't be intimidated. "Yes. That's what I said. Bluffing."

"I don't bluff, and what I did was test you." His dark eyes burned. "You failed."

"I'm not surprised," she flashed. "And just a little FYI, it's hard to feel sympathy for you, or your causes, when you so blatantly disregard other people's needs and feelings."

"You have no idea who or what you're dealing with, do you?"

She did, actually. He was a bandit and a kidnapper and it wouldn't be wise to push him too far but she was so angry now she wasn't thinking straight. "You don't test people."

"Of course you do. It's smart. It's strategy. One must know others strengths and weaknesses."

"And you think you know mine?"

"I know you're not to be trusted." His lips compressed, and he looked hard, knowing, controlled. "But then, few people can be."

She looked away, eyes burning and for some reason this last trickery hurt more than anything. He'd manipulated her all along. Played her. But it wasn't just what he'd done, it was his attitude that hurt. "You have a terrible way of looking at life."

"It's practical. It keeps me, and my people, alive."

A voice spoke from outside and then the tent flap was pushed aside and the elderly man from last night appeared with a large breakfast tray heaped with fresh and dried fruits, a mound of round, flat flour-dusted breads, and steaming cups of mint tea. The man disappeared as soon as he placed the tray on the carpet in front of the bed.

Her captor motioned to the carpet. "You'll join me," he said, and it wasn't a question or invitation but an order.

"I'm not hungry." She was still seething over the loss of all her photos. So much work. It was a loss of devastating proportions.

"You need to eat," he answered with a snap of his fingers. He jabbed downward to the ground, pointing at the carpet.

"I've never met a ruder Berber man," she muttered under

her breath but she knew he heard—and understood—from the look he gave her.

He took one of the small flat breads. "There are worse."

She watched him eat, eyes burning, head throbbing. She did need to eat, as well as drink, but she was afraid of getting sick, and at the moment her nervous system felt as though it were in overdrive. "What do I have to do to get my pictures back?"

"I don't wish to discuss this topic anymore."

"It's important—"

"Not anymore. You're not taking pictures here."

"So what will I do while I'm here?"

He looked at her for a long, tense moment, his expression blank, dark eyes guarded, shadowed. "Nothing."

"Nothing?"

His broad shoulders shifted carelessly. "I'm not going to make you do anything. I'm perfectly content now that I have your film to wait."

"Wait for what?"

"The truth. It will emerge. It always does."

"Maybe, but it could take a long time."

"Indeed. And if that is the case, you'll get to enjoy desert life for an indefinite period of time."

"Indefinite."

"Unless you care to tell me the truth now, Woman?"

"I've told you the truth and my name isn't Woman, it's Tally."

"I've never heard the name Tally before. That's not a name." A glint of light touched his dark eyes, something secret and perverse and then the corner of his mouth nearly lifted, the closest thing she'd seen to a smile yet. "I shall call you Woman."

She didn't know if it was his words, his tone or that perverse light in his eyes but it annoyed her almost beyond reason. "I won't answer to it."

"You will."

"I won't."

"You will." And more fire flashed in his eyes. "Even if it takes days. Weeks." He hesitated, and his dark gaze slid over her, the first openly assessing look he'd given her, one that examined, weighed, understood. "Years."

Heat stormed her cheeks. The same heat that flooded her veins. "*Not* years."

"You will answer to me one day, Woman. You might not like the idea, but it's true. The sooner you accept it, the sooner life will become easier for you."

She wanted to throw something at him, anything. The cups of tea. The tray. A pillow. He was so damn smug. So horribly arrogant. "I take it then I call you Man?"

His faint smile faded. "You are very impertinent for a woman." Silent, he regarded her. "You may call me Tair," he said after a moment.

"Why do you get a name and I get Woman?"

"Because I brought you here, which makes you my responsibility, and therefore my woman."

"That doesn't make sense."

"It does to me and that's all that matters since this is my tribe and you are mine."

"Will you please stop calling me your woman? I'm not your woman. I'm no one's woman, and I wasn't spying on you or whatever you think I was doing in El Saroush's medina," she said, referring to the border town's old square where he'd kidnapped her. "Why would I spy on you? I don't even know who you are, and what point would there be spying on a group of bedraggled men riding through town on horseback? I may be an American," and she drawled the word for his benefit, "but I do have standards."

He nearly hissed. "Bedraggled men?"

She crossed her arms, chin titled rebelliously. "Even your horses are bedraggled."

"They're not," he contradicted, incensed. "Our horses are

some of the finest Arabians in North Africa. We breed them ourselves."

"They're dirty. You're all dirty—"

"You should see yourself."

"I'd bathe if you let me! I'd love some clean clothes, too, but somehow I don't think you kidnapped a change of clothes for me."

"I'll get a knife," he muttered, "get rid of your damn tongue now."

She should be afraid, she should, but somehow she wasn't. He might be huge, and fierce and intimidating but he didn't seem cruel, or like a man who impulsively cut out tongues. "The point is that I didn't even notice you in town. I was interested only in the children playing. And all I want to do is be allowed to continue on to Casablanca."

"Why Casablanca?"

"It's the next stop on my itinerary."

His expression turned speculative. "You've friends there?"

"No. I'm on my own."

"Casablanca's a rebel stronghold."

Tally sighed. "You're rather obsessive about this whole terrorist thing, aren't you?"

He studied her for a long moment before leaning forward to take her face in his hand. He lifted her chin this way and then that. "You are what, thirty years old? Older?"

She tried to pull away but couldn't. Her pulse jumped, skin burning. She didn't like him touching her. He made her feel odd, prickly things. Things she had no business feeling. "I just turned thirty," she answered faintly.

"You wear no ring," he said, still examining her face. "Did your husband die?"

"I've never been married."

"Never?"

"I don't want a husband."

He let her go then and his dense black lashes dropped, concealing his expression. He was silent, assessing her, and the situation. "You're not a virgin, are you?"

His tone had changed and she didn't know if it was shock, or respect but either way it irritated her. Her life, her past, her relationships, and most of all, her sexuality were her business and no one else's. Least of all a barbaric desert tribesman. "I'm thirty, not thirteen. Of course I've had relationships—and experience—but I choose to remain single. I prefer being single. This way I can travel. Explore. Do what I want to do."

Tair continued to study her as though she were alien and fascinating in a strange sort of way.

Tally wasn't sure she liked the look on his face. His expression made her nervous. Made her feel painfully vulnerable.

"Your parents—they're still alive?" he asked.

She nodded, neck stiff, body rigid. She really didn't know where he was going with this and didn't want to find out.

"They don't worry about you?" he persisted.

"No." She caught his eye, flushed. "Maybe a little. But they're used to my lifestyle now. They know this is who I am, what I do. Besides, they have other kids who supply them with grandchildren and the like."

Tair refilled his cup of tea from the small glazed pot. "I shall find you a husband."

"What?"

He nodded matter of factly before sipping his tea. "You need a husband. It is the way it should be. I shall find you one. You will be glad."

"No." Her head spun, little spots danced before her eyes. He wrong, absolutely wrong and she couldn't even get the protest out. Instead she sucked in one desperate breath after another.

"Women are like fruit," he said picking up a date, gently squeezing it. "Women need husbands and children or they dry up."

Dry up? He didn't just say that. He didn't say that while

squeezing a little date, did he? My God. This was a nightmare. This was worse than anything she could have ever imagined, and she'd imagined some pretty awful endings. Kidnapped, her photos stripped from her and now what? Married to a desert barbarian? "Let me go home. Please correct this before it turns out badly."

"I will make sure you have the right husband. Do not worry." His lips curved and she saw teeth, straight white teeth and thought this must be his idea of a smile. "Now eat. Berber men like women with meat on their bones. Curves. Not stringy like you."

Tally went hot and cold. She felt wild, panicked. She couldn't be here, couldn't stay here. This was all wrong. Wrong, wrong, wrong.

Tair sighed, frowned. "You must at least drink the tea. You're dehydrated. I can see it in your eyes and skin."

Tally wasn't a crier but she was close to tears now. How was she going to do this? Would she escape?

"You don't like tea?" he persisted, the strain on his patience showing. "Would you prefer water?"

"Is it bottled water?"

His black brows tugged together. "It's well water."

"But not processed?" She'd only just gotten off of weeks of wretched antibiotics, antibiotics that were proved to be just as hard on her stomach as the parasite and food poisoning. Just remembering the forty-eight hours in the Atiq hospital made her stomach cramp. "You see I can't drink water that isn't purified. I've had problems—"

"You are without a doubt the most delicate, finicky female I've ever met."

"I'm not finicky and not overly delicate—"

"Asthma, heat stroke, stomach ailments, dehydration—"

"I didn't ask to be kidnapped! This was your idea not mine. If you don't like that I'm so delicate, next time do more research before you kidnap a woman!"

He shook his head, expression grim. "You are not going to make it easy for me to find you a husband. Men do not like mulish wives."

Mulish. Mulish, was she? Tally nearly laughed. That was rich, coming from him. "You know, you have a very good vocabulary for a desert bandit."

"I like to read between making raids on towns." He snapped his fingers. "Now drink. None of my men will marry a woman if she's nearly dead."

"I don't want your men."

"How you love to argue."

"I have my own opinions and point of view, and contrary to what you might think, I'm not normally difficult. You just happen to bring out the worst in me." She glared at him. "Until yesterday, I hadn't had an asthma attack in years. The attack was thanks to you nearly suffocating me in that horrible bag of yours. I can't believe you did that. It was terrible. Awful. I couldn't breathe."

"So I noticed." His brow lowered, his expression dark. "But you were quiet at least."

She covered her face with her hands, breathing in carefully, deliberately, doing her best to block out the smell of the mint tea, the peculiar sandalwood scent and smoke of Tair's skin, and the intense heat already shimmering all around them. She couldn't do another day in the desert. Not like this. Not with this man.

She was near tears and cracking. "Can you please go? Can you please just leave me alone?"

He didn't answer. He was so quiet that after a minute Tally was certain he'd gone but when she lifted her head she saw him there, still seated across from her. He didn't look the least bit sympathetic, either. If anything, his jaw jutted harder, his mouth pursed in a now familiar look of judgment and condescension.

"Drink your tea," he said wearily. "This is the desert, and

the heat is quite deceptive. You need to stay hydrated or you won't live long enough to take another picture, much less visit Casablanca." His dark eyes gleamed as he pushed a cup toward her face. "Which is overrated, if you ask me."

Her eyebrows arched. Was that a joke? Was that flat tone and deadpan expression his idea of a joke? "I don't trust the water," she retorted, pushing the cup away. "And yes, I am thirsty, and I will drink. But it must be bottled water."

"Bottled water?"

She ignored his incredulous tone. He didn't understand the difficulties she'd had these past four weeks. She'd never had a cast iron stomach but it'd become particularly finicky lately ever since she picked up parasites from local water just outside Atiq. The parasites had her practically sleeping in the bathroom and she had no interest repeating that experience again. "Yes, bottled water. You sell it in the stores."

A small muscle popped in his jaw as he gave her a ferocious look, one that revealed the depth of his irritation and aggravation. "And you see stores near by?"

"No, but there were stores back in El Saroush."

"Are you suggesting I send someone back for bottled water?"

"I'm suggesting you send someone back with me."

He sighed heavily and pressed two fingers to his temple. "You have the most tedious refrain."

Her lips compressed. He might not realize it, but she was just as irritated and frustrated as he was. "I've only just begun."

"I should just cut out your tongue."

"You wouldn't want to do that," she flashed. "My new husband might not like it."

"That's true," he answered. "He might miss it, and it could lower your bride price. So, keep your tongue and drink your tea. Or I shall pour it down your throat."

The cup was pushed toward her face again and this time Tally took it. "If I drink the tea, you'll leave?"

His dark gaze met hers and held. The corner of his mouth lifted, a faint wry acknowledgment of the battle between them. "Yes."

And yet still she hesitated. "And if I die out here of dysentery, will you at least promise me a Christian burial?"

The corner of his mouth twitched. "I can't promise that, but I will take your ashes to Casablanca."

Tally wasn't sure if she should be reassured or troubled by his faint smile. He wasn't a particularly smiley-kind of guy. "Fine, I'll drink it. But then you go." Quickly she downed the now lukewarm tea, scrunching her nose and mouth at the bitter taste but at the same time grateful for the liquid. Her throat had been parched and one cup wasn't going to be enough, but it was a start. "There. Done."

He rose, but didn't leave immediately. Instead he stood above her, gazing down at her. "By the way, we may be bedraggled barbarians and bandits, but all our water is boiled. Any water we cook with or drink is always boiled. You might get parasites in town, but you won't get any parasites from me."

And smiling—smiling!—Tair walked out. As he left the tent, Tally grabbed a pillow, pressed it to her face and screamed in vexation.

He couldn't keep her here! He couldn't. And he couldn't be serious about finding a husband for her. My God. That was just the worst.

She gripped the pillow hard. But what if he never returned her to town? What if he just kept her here? What if he were serious about marrying her off?

She shuddered, appalled.

Her lack of communication with her world back in the States made her situation doubly frightening.

The fact was, there was no one who'd even think to worry if she disappeared from the face of the earth.

Raised in a tiny town at the base of the Cascade Mountains in Washington, Tally had lived at home far longer than she'd ever meant to stay but once she'd left North Bend, she'd gone far away.

Her mother sometimes joked that the only time she heard from Tally was the annual Christmas cards Tally sent documenting her travels. One Christmas card was a misty hand-tinted shot of ancient Machu Picchu high in the mountains of Peru. Another year it was the sun rising in Antarctica. Last year's card was a child born with AIDS in sub-Sahara Africa.

Once Paolo was the one who would have cared. It was Paolo who taught her to rock climb and sail, Paolo who'd taught her to face her fears and not be afraid. But Paolo wasn't around anymore and since losing him all those years ago Tally had never tried to replace him.

Love hadn't ever come easily for Tally and one broken heart was more than enough. And not that she would have married Paolo, but if she'd wanted a husband—and that was a huge *if*—it would have been him. And only him. But with him gone, marriage was out of the question.

Tossing aside the pillow, Tally forced herself to eat even as she struggled to remember who she last spoke with, whom she'd written, and the last e-mails she'd sent from the Internet café in Atiq a month ago.

Did anyone even know she was still in Northern Africa? Her editor might, but they hadn't communicated in weeks.

No, keeping in touch wasn't her forte. While she loved taking pictures, she didn't like writing and most of her e-mails were brief one-liners. *In Israel, went diving in the Red Sea.* Or, *Arrived in Pakistan, took a bus through Harappa, have never been so hot in my entire life.*

Tally now stared glumly at the breakfast tray. She was going to pay for her laissez-faire attitude, wasn't she?

The older man was outside her tent again, calling to her, saying something she didn't understand as he spoke with an accent or in a dialect she'd never heard before. But before she could answer, he'd entered the tent, carrying a relatively large copper tub. He placed the tub on the carpet, indicated that he'd go and return and when he returned he had help. Three men carried pitchers of water.

A bath.

So something she'd said to Tair had sunk in. Thrilled, Tally watched as the elderly man filled the tub with the pitchers of steaming water and left behind a soft soap and towel. The bath wasn't particularly deep, and not exactly hot, but it was warm water and she had a bar of soap, a soap that reminded her of olive oil and citrus. She washed her hair, soaped up and down and by the time she rinsed off, the water was cold but she felt marvelous. Marvelous until she realized she had nothing but her dirty clothes to put back on.

Regretfully Tally dressed in her clothes, combed her fingers through her hair, pulling the wet strands back from her face and then looked around the tent. She was sick of the tent. She'd been here for not even a day and she already hated it.

So enough of the tent. She was heading out to explore the camp.

From the moment she pushed the goatskin flap up and exited her tent, stepping into the startling bright sunlight, Tally became aware of the eyes of the men in camp on her. It was obvious they didn't approve of her wandering around but no one made a move toward her. No one spoke to her and no one detained her. They pretty much let her do as she pleased.

The camp was actually bigger than it first appeared. There were over a dozen tents, and several large open ones with scattered rugs and pillows and Tally guessed these were the places the men gathered to eat and socialize.

A mangy three-legged dog hopped around after her and Tally considered discouraging the dog but then decided she liked the company. And it was her first friend.

Crouching down, Tally scratched under the dog's chin and

then behind one ear. "If I had my camera working, I'd take a picture of you." The dog wagged its tail that looked half gnawed. "Poor dog. You look just as bad as this camp does."

And the camp did look bad. She'd never seen anything like this place. It was poor. Stark. Depressing. And once again she thought she'd give anything to have one of the memory cards back because she'd love to photograph the camp. The stained tents with the backdrop of sand dunes and kneeling camels would make amazing pictures.

Suddenly she heard a now familiar voice—the old Berber man—and he was running toward her with long cotton fabric draped over his arm.

Tally didn't know what he was saying but once he unfurled one of the strips of fabric and she saw it was a robe she knew he wanted her to cover up.

"No, thank you," she said, shaking her hands and head. "I'm fine."

But he insisted and the more he insisted the more adamant Tally was that she wouldn't wear the black robe and head covering. "No," she said more firmly, even as she began to wonder just where Tair was. She'd walked the circumference of the camp twice without spotting him once.

"Tair," she said to the old man. "Where is he?"

The old man stared at her uncomprehendingly. Then he lifted the robe, shook it. She knew what he wanted but he didn't understand what she did.

"Tair," Tally repeated and this time she stood on her toes, lifted her hand high above her head to indicate Tair's immense height. *"Tair."*

The elderly man only looked more puzzled and Tally wanted to pull her hair out in mad chunks. This was a nightmare. A nightmare. She couldn't stay here, couldn't be left here, couldn't. Wouldn't.

"Tair," she said more loudly, firmly, extending her arms to show width, size.

The old man just looked at her with absolute incomprehension.

It was at that moment she spotted the horse. The horse was saddled, bridled and unattended.

Unattended.

She could just go.

It wasn't logical, nothing rational about her plan. She was just going to go and she didn't know anything other than to go, just go, and let the chips fall where they may.

She climbed up, onto the blanket that served as the saddle and taking the reins she kicked at the horse, urging him to go.

The horse gave her a funny sideways glance before stretching out in an easy canter. They rode across the pale creamy sand at a quick clip, Tally's heart racing at the same speed they were traveling.

This was crazy, foolish, dangerous. But she didn't turn back and didn't slow. She felt as if she were running for her very life. Or make that, running from her very life.

She wouldn't be trapped again. She wouldn't let others control her life or her destiny.

She'd had years of answering to others, years of giving up her own hopes, years of waiting and she couldn't wait any more.

With the dazzling sun shining in her eyes and the heat exploding all around them, Tally tried to get a better grip, the blanket style saddle unfamiliar. Part of her brain told her to slow down and another part was just wild—frenzied—and she simply kept going at that reckless, breakneck speed.

Maybe if she'd had a different past, a different experience with life, she could sit in the camp and wait. But she wasn't good at waiting, not when she felt as though she'd spent her whole life waiting.

Tally wasn't an only child. In fact, she was far from an only, being the eldest in a family of five children. She'd been responsible for so much. She'd been responsible for well, virtually everything.

From an early age Tally walked her younger brothers and sisters to and from school, fed and clothed them when their mother had to return to work after their father's back injury put him virtually to bed for the rest of his life. Tally oversaw homework, meals, shopping, laundry, cleaning. If one of the youngest needed a parent for Open House or Back to School Night it was Tally who showed up more often than Mom.

As a teenager Tally used to dream about leaving home, about the day she'd pack everything into her car and just go— flee the pressure and responsibilities—but by the time she graduated from high school her mother's health was in decline and Tally knew she couldn't go. Couldn't walk away from the younger ones who wanted her, or her parents who needed her.

Instead of escaping in real life, she escaped in her mind, using books and movies, theater and photography to go places she couldn't go in person. The Amazon? She was there! Everest? She climbed it! Egypt? On the next camel. Paris? Bring on the Eiffel Tower.

It wasn't until the youngest one, her brother Jude, started high school that she allowed herself to dream of actually going away. But when fifteen-year-old Jude turned sixteen and earned his driver's license and made Varsity on the football team she realized the baby Deavers was old enough, big enough and strong enough to take care of himself.

Her parents begged her not to go, pleaded that they still needed her but Tally was nearly twenty-six, had never been anywhere, had done nothing for the past ten years but take care of everyone else and she was going to go now. She'd have her turn. Even if it killed her.

And staring at the huge expanse of desert with sand and sand and more sand Tally realized her need for her turn might just kill her, too.

What the hell was she doing in Baraka—or Ouaha, or wherever she was at the moment—anyway?

Tally didn't know if she slipped, or the horse stumbled, but one moment she was on the horse, and the next, she'd somehow lost her balance and was falling. Tally tumbled to the ground even as the horse continued on.

The fall knocked the air from her but the burning sand quickly roused her.

Gasping, she dragged herself to her feet, wincing at the pain in her side. Oh, that hurt.

Eyes damp, she lifted a trembling hand and brushed the grains of sand from her cheek and collar. For a moment she felt a surge of panic, but just as quickly she smothered it. She wasn't going to panic. She was going to be strong. Tears wouldn't help. Just determination. And lots of resolve.

Gathering her resolve, Tally set off, heading in the same direction the horse had gone. It was relatively easy following the horse's hoofprints.

Ignoring the blistering sun, she walked on. This is what she'd done the past five years, she reminded herself. Ever since she left home she'd been living with a knapsack slung on her back, traveling to the most remote corners of the world, photographing the children time seemed to have forgotten.

Tally had never really examined why she'd become a children's photographer. Yes, it was the first work she'd gotten in Seattle, but why babies and toddlers? Why leggy little girls and wide-eyed boys torn between childhood and adolescent?

And with the glimpse of swirling sand darkening the horizon Tally realized it wasn't by accident. She photographed the faces of children to learn her own.

There'd been no real childhood for her. No time to indulge in play. No fantasy and fancy, no dress up, no costumes, no baton lessons or classes of gymnastics and ballet. No ice skating—*where would the money come from, honey? Besides we need you here.*

A lump filled Tally's throat but she didn't dwell on the emotion, not when the horizon seemed to turn black before her very eyes.

Just moments ago the horizon had looked dark, muddy with swirling sand but it wasn't muddy anymore. It looked eerie, frightening.

Her steps faltered. With her heart in her throat she realized she was walking straight into a sandstorm.

CHAPTER FOUR

TALLY turned, looked behind her, wondering where she could go, how she could protect herself. But there was nowhere to go. And as she watched, the cloud and wind of sand grew, stretching from her feet far overhead as if even the sky was made of beige and brown. The pale sun disappeared and the afternoon grew ominously still.

Goose bumps covered Tally's arms and lifted the hair at her nape. She felt the danger, felt the heaviness in the sky, the weighty silence of impending doom. The sandstorm was growing, building, billowing like a sci-fi monster come to life.

There was no sound anywhere. No sound of anything but the stillness of the desert and yet to Tally it was like a roar, a scream. The sand monster breathes, she thought, wrapping her arms around her upper body, fingers pressing tightly against her skin as the blackness sailed toward her.

I'm going to perish here. This is where it ends. And I don't even have my camera.

She tried to laugh at her feeble humor in the face of abject terror but her laugh was a hiccup and her gaze clung sickeningly to the huge black whirling wall of sand very nearly on her now.

This is it. This is all. This is how it ends.

And then from nowhere came the sound of hooves, fast furious thudding hooves and turning Tally saw a blur of horse and man as Tair on his flying black horse raced toward her, leaning low on his stallion's back and with one arm he scooped her up, lifting her onto his saddle in front of him. And he never slowed, not even to grab her, or settle her. Instead he pushed her low against the horse's neck and he dropped his body over hers urging his stallion on, and they were running for their lives, running against sand and storm and monsters shaped from the vengeful desert wind.

They were riding toward a rock that protruded from the land, something Tally had seen only from afar and had never thought twice about but now that they were closer she could see crevices in the rock, openings like little caves and Tair rode there now. The wind storm with its pelting sand began to bite at their skin, sharp cuts and stings and Tally covered her mouth and nose to keep from sucking the sand in.

"Get in," Tair shouted above the storm's roar. He half-dropped, half-tossed her toward the cleft in the rock and as terrified as she was of scorpions and snakes she knew they were a safer option.

Tally crawled swiftly in, and Tair followed, dragging his horse's head in after him, holding the reins tightly so his stallion couldn't escape.

With the sharp rock pressed to her back and Tair pressed to her front Tally closed her eyes and listened to the howling storm outside.

If Tair hadn't come…

If Tair hadn't gone in search of her…

And her eyes burned, and despite her tightly closed lids she could feel small hot tears prick and sting, could feel her throat squeeze.

This was not the way she liked to live life.

This was not her life.

She was going to have adventures, yes, and she'd see the world, but it'd be her way. In her time. She'd explore and venture out but she wouldn't have to rely on anyone.

Wouldn't be dependent on anyone.

Wouldn't need anything from anyone, either.

Tair's horse shook his head unhappily several times, shifting from foot to foot as the howling outside became a shrieking crescendo.

"Your horse is unhappy," she said, feeling the stallion's discomfort, knowing the pelting sand must be biting through his hide.

"He's not the only one unhappy," Tair said tersely.

It was dark in the cavern, and yet tilting her head back she could just make out Tair's hard features but they didn't appear harsh as much as set. Fixed. Determined.

She swallowed, painfully aware of him and the press of their bodies. He rested his weight on his arms, tried to keep his body from crushing hers and yet even without him touching her, she could imagine how his hands would feel against her skin, could see his fingertips trail slowly down her spine.

Oh, it'd be hot.

It'd burn her up.

Tally felt desire curl in her belly and heat wash through every limb. Her body shook and she wondered if Tair could feel it.

Balling her hands into fists, she tried to intellectualize what she was feeling, dissect the attraction and rationalize it was fear, adrenaline. These things happened. Paolo had even said that many men and women fell in love with each other in the midst of dangerous situations, something about raised hormones and chemical surges.

It's the danger, she told herself, feeling the tension between her and Tair. It's the storm and the noise, the pelting sand and the intense heat inside the cave making everything extreme. I'm not attracted to him. Can't be.

"How did you sleep last night?" Tair asked, raising his voice to be heard over the howling sand devil.

She stiffened beneath him. "Like hell, and you know it."

His mouth curved and with one hand he lazily pushed her thick hair back from her face. "You put on quite a show last night. Everyone could hear you. My men were most fascinated."

Tally jumped at the brush of his fingers, so sensitive that just that fleeting touch made her tremble. "I'm glad I could provide them with some entertainment."

His smile broadened. He'd shaven this morning and his jaw was clean, a hard polished bronze, which accented the height of his cheekbone and his strong aristocratic nose. "Your future husband will have his hands full with you."

She averted her face, stared at the rough sandstone wall. "I'm not interested."

The horse shifted, moved forward, nudging Tair and his body pressed against hers. Tally shivered at the press of his hips and chest.

"I am sure we will find one man here who can manage you. Clearly it will take a special man—"

"I'm not amused," she answered breathlessly, feeling trapped, panicked. He was so solid, and yet warm and it confused her. The same way her attraction confused her. She couldn't want him. It was illogical. Everything about this was crazy. He was a man wedded to the desert while she craved freedom, freedom and adventure.

Freedom. And this, she thought, stricken as his body touched hers in every place it shouldn't, wasn't freedom.

She couldn't live in his world here and to even be tempted by him, to even be tempted to want someone like him spoke of disaster.

With an unsteady hand she pressed her fingers to her brow and closed her eyes, willing herself to ignore him. Forget him. The cave might be small and his body might be torturing hers but she'd been in more dangerous situations than this. She could survive this. She just had to stay calm.

And then the horse shifted again and Tair's right knee went forward, sliding between her own and she felt his warm hard thigh slide against her, felt the heat and sinewy strength against her where she was so sensitive, where every nerve ending screamed for increased sensation and it was shocking. Disturbing. Arousing.

She opened her mouth to gasp, her mind protesting the intimacy even as her body wanted more but the sound was swallowed by the wild roar outside.

Inwardly she cursed the desert and its oppressive heat as well as the wretched Berber tribesman who took her.

Wildly, she looked up, caught Tair's eye.

The wretched man was smiling. "Perhaps with the right man you will grow to like it here with us," he said, voice low, taunting. "Perhaps you will never want to go back to America."

Tally couldn't answer. Never return? Live here in his encampment? With a shake of her head, she turned her face away, squeezed her eyes shut and tried to think of other places, other people.

She wouldn't remain here. Wouldn't belong to a Berber. Never. Ever.

Ever.

Tally didn't know how long they lay there, huddled in the crevice, the air so hot, stifling that sweat dribbled down her neck, between her breasts, her skin damp, the air stagnant and old.

But finally the noise outside faded and the stallion shook his head again, pulling at the reins and this time Tair loosened his grip allowing his horse to slowly back up. Tally got a glimpse of blue sky. The storm had passed.

They climbed from the cave, and Tally slowly straightened, limbs achy and tight. Tair tossed her onto the saddle and jumped behind her and with a shake of the bridle let the horse run, and they were off, cantering toward the encampment.

"Are your men all right?" Tally finally dared to ask as she spotted tents ahead, sand piled high against the sides. "The sandstorm won't have hurt them?"

"They're fine," he said curtly, reining his horse in. "You're the one in danger."

Men surged around them as they dismounted and Tair brusquely answered several of the men even as he hauled her through the crowd to his tent.

In his tent he thrust her down onto the low chair that faced a simple desk.

"Have you lost your mind?" he roared, planting himself before her, hands on his hips. "What do you think you were doing?"

Tally clenched her hands in her lap. "Running away!"

"It was stupid."

"Keeping me here is worse."

"No. Keeping you here is keeping you safe. And I won't have you running off, putting yourself in danger, making my men chase after you. It's time you learned to stay put. Act like a woman your age."

"Why do you keep bringing up my age?"

"Because you're not a child. You're a woman of childbearing age—"

"Leave my age out of it!"

"I can't."

"Why not? It's none of your business. Nothing I do is any of your business."

"You're wrong about that. Everything you do in my country is my business." He pulled up a second low stool and sat down directly in front of her, but even sitting he was a full head and shoulders taller, and even sitting he towered over her. "And where were you going anyway?"

She tried to rock back on her chair hating his close proximity. With his dark hair coated with grit and sand, and sand in his black eyebrows he looked wild. Instead of a pirate on a ship, he was a pirate of the desert. "To get help," she answered coldly.

"Help?"

"Police, or protection—"

"Protection from who?" he roared.

"You!"

He threw up his hands. "I protect you. I saved you from the rebels. I saved you from violent people."

"I'm sorry, Tair, but you're the only dangerous man I've met in Northern Africa!"

He made a rough sound of disgust. "And just who is going to give you this protection from me?"

"The government of Ouaha."

"The government," he repeated, giving her a look she couldn't decipher even as he shook his head. "I am the government."

She didn't like the look in his eye or the smugness at his mouth. "You're chief of the desert."

"Yes."

"But surely there is someone else higher than you…someone with more authority."

He just looked at her.

Tally's heart and stomach seemed to be in direct collision and it made her very very nauseous. "Isn't there a sultan of Ouaha? A king? Someone higher than a sheikh?"

If he heard the panic in her voice he gave no indication. "There is one that holds the title Sultan of Ouaha, but he isn't one of our people. He is a Berber sheikh from Baraka and he and his family have befriended Ouaha, but they have no power here."

"But you do answer to him?"

"I answer to no one."

Reason, not emotion, reason, not emotion she chanted to herself but it wasn't helping. "But if I went to him, this Sultan who is Barakan, he would help me, wouldn't he? He would free me. He wouldn't allow you to keep me, an American woman, hostage here."

"First, you will not be able to speak to Sheikh Nuri as he lives in London and you don't have the means to get there.

And second, even if you should speak to him, he wouldn't go against my wishes. We have fought too many wars together, protected each other's backs too many times. He trusts my judgment. I trust his."

"So how long do you intend to keep me here?"

Tair shrugged. "Forever?"

"You're going to feed and clothe me forever? Very generous of you."

He shrugged again. "Not that generous. You might not live very long. The desert is a dangerous place."

"A threat?"

"I don't threaten. No need. My word here is law. Anything I want, I get."

"Must feel pretty wonderful."

The corner of his mouth lifted ever so slightly and yet his gaze remained just as flat, hard, unfriendly. "It's not a boast. Just a fact."

"So what exactly do you do? What are the job descriptions of a sheikh?"

"Think of it as a mini-kingdom."

"And you are the king?"

"Exactly. I make the final decisions. And now I decide its time for you to bathe and return to your tent where you will behave the way a woman should."

Alone in his tent, Tair bathed, soaping up and washing his hair before toweling off and changing into clean trousers and a loose overshirt. He slicked his wet hair back from his brow.

He was going to have to do something about the American. After what happened today there was talk in the camp, a great deal of talk, and most of it was about her.

Tair didn't like the talk, or the speculation about the kind of woman she was, or how she'd be in bed. In his culture men didn't discuss women—unless they were foreign women and then the assumption was that they were up for grabs.

Tair folded back the cuffs on his shirt and then stood to watch the setting sun paint the desert shades of crimson and gold.

In his culture women married young to protect their reputations. If a woman remained single too long no one would believe she'd remained a virgin, and in Ouaha, a woman's virginity—her purity—was her greatest asset.

Tair realized Tally wasn't of his culture, and he was familiar with her Western thought and education, but she was here now, living among his people, his men. He had to do what was right. To protect her. To ensure no one exploited her. And he knew just how to solve the problem.

Tally paced her tent in an absolute temper. She wouldn't bathe. Wouldn't change. Wouldn't do anything she was told. She'd do what she wanted to do, and only what she wanted to do. Period.

Back and forth she went over the old carpet, footsteps muffled by the soft handwoven wool.

He could say he'd lock her up. He could threaten isolation. Starvation. Fine. It'd make a great book someday. She'd become a bestseller. Maybe she'd even win a big literary prize.

Tally glared at the tent opening where the flap had been tied back, in case she tried to run away. *In case.* Huh. How about, for *when* she ran away again.

Now she glared at the undulating sand dunes in the distance and the men crouched in a circle by the black fire pit.

She didn't care if Tair was sheikh, or king, or emperor of the whole damn desert. He'd hate keeping her here. She'd be a horrible captive. She'd make his life miserable. He had to know it.

Furiously, restlessly, she kicked at the carpet covering the sand. My God she was going crazy here. But better to be angry than helpless.

Anger was a much better emotion than fear, than doubt. Years ago she'd made a vow—with Paolo's help, of course—

to face every fear with action. And confronting her fears had worked. Look at all the things she'd done: climbed treacherous mountains, kayaked in shark-infested seas, learned to fly solo. All because she'd once been afraid of danger. And change.

Now look at her. Captive in the desert, held hostage by Sheikh Tair el-Tayer, or whatever he called himself.

If only she could stay calm, really calm, not just on the outside but on the inside. Unfortunately, on the inside right now she was a hellcat, all anger and hissing sound and claws. But sometimes anger wasn't a bad thing. Sometimes, anger protected, empowered. Anger got things done.

Tally exhaled slowly. Okay, maybe in this case anger wasn't going to accomplish anything. Maybe anger was just going to make life worse.

She dropped onto her low bed, flung her arms over her head, stared up at the roof of her tent. He had to let her go. Send her back. He had to.

Minutes crept by. Endlessly long minutes. Tally yawned. Wiggled. Shrugged her shoulders, stretching.

The sun still wasn't down yet. The night would be endless. She'd be alone and going crazy again.

If only he'd just give her one memory card. Let her do something. Let her photograph the sky, the dunes, the sunsets. She needed activity, needed to keep her mind occupied. If she didn't find a way to stay busy she'd lose it for certain.

She was bored. And worse, lonely. Tally hated being lonely, hated that awful empty feeling she got inside.

Even Tair's horrible company would be better right now than no company.

She slammed her fists on either side of her, hitting the bed's mattress hard. She couldn't do this. Couldn't handle this. She was bored and mad and ready to explode.

"You should try meditation." Tair's deep voice, tinged with amusement, broke the stillness.

Tally sat up swiftly. "Meditation?"

"It'd help," he added kindly, the fading sunset behind him shot with lavender and purple streaks.

She hated the sudden leap inside her, a funny twitchy feeling in her chest, matched by a flutter in her stomach. Disgusting, she thought. She *was* glad to see him. "Help how?"

He smiled idly, as if enjoying her temper. "You're the least peaceful person I've ever met."

How could he enjoy her misery? What kind of man was he? "I don't want to be peaceful, Sheikh Tair. I *want* to leave."

"But you're not going to leave so you might as well learn to relax." He entered the tent, spotted the tub of water and stack of soap and towels that hadn't been touched. "You haven't bathed."

"I wasn't in the mood."

"You like being dirty?"

Tally was just about to make another comment on the squalor of his encampment but decided better of it at the last moment. "If you'll give me some privacy, I'll bathe now."

"I'll give you five minutes—"

"Why so little?"

"Because dinner is on the way and tonight I'm having dinner with you."

Tally took a very fast bath, not just because she only had five minutes to bathe and change, but because the water had cooled and a chilly bath wasn't her idea of fun.

Dressed, Tally was just combing her damp hair when Tair's elderly servant arrived with dinner.

Tally sat down across from Tair in her tent, the lantern tonight replaced with three fat flickering candles. The meal was simple, stew and a couscous and some flat bread, but she was hungry and ate virtually everything.

She looked up to find Tair watching her and his expression with its hard features, and firm proud mouth, softened with a half smile. "It's good to see you eat," he said.

"That's right. You think I'm stringy."

He had the grace to make a face, laughing at himself. "You didn't like that."

"No, I didn't."

He laughed softly now. "You are so feisty. Everything is a battle with you."

"I just have opinions of my own."

"So I've noticed." But he wasn't angry. He sounded almost…indulgent.

Their gazes locked, and she felt her face burn and darken, as a rush of heat swept through her cheeks. Impulsively she leaned forward, over the small table with the flickering candles. "Can we try this again?" she asked. "Can we try to start over?"

Tair leaned back, reclining against the pillows behind him. "Why would we want to start over?"

"Get a fresh start. Things haven't gone well and I thought it'd behoove us both—"

"Behoove?" he interrupted, dark eyes gleaming, and a single black eyebrow rising to mock her. "I haven't heard that word in years. Didn't realize it was still part of the English language."

Tally felt her jaw clench. How quickly he could kill her good moods. "I don't see why it shouldn't be used. It's a wonderful word."

"Indeed, it is."

Her hand squeezed the cup of mint tea she'd been holding. Why did she think she enjoyed his company? Why had she even missed him earlier?

"The point," she said carefully, trying to sidestep her profound—and growing—resentment, "is that we haven't gotten off on the best footing and I think it'd be good if we tried again. Started over. Formed new first impressions."

"Why?"

She couldn't seem to escape the intensity in his expression, his dark eyes fierce, demanding, insistent. And while he wasn't touching her, she felt the heat again grow between them, matching the heat growing within her.

"I don't understand you," she said, swallowing hard, trying to calm her racing heart. She'd never win an argument with Tair by getting emotional. He was reason, and logic. "I don't understand anything about you."

"What do you need to understand?"

Helplessly Tally searched his face. "I've told you I'm a photographer. I've told you I work for no one but myself. You've even had the chance to see my photos but it doesn't seem to matter to you. You refuse to help me and only you can."

"But I have helped you," he answered calmly. "I will always help you."

"How?" she demanded, genuinely perplexed. This was probably a cultural thing, some distance between East and West, but he had to realize she wasn't one of his women. She'd never be a Berber woman.

"And for that matter," he continued, not bothering to answer her question but finish making his point, "why would we want to start over, or try to form new impressions, when what we know might be true?"

"But maybe it isn't the truth. Maybe you have some idea of me that I'm not—"

"I don't think so."

Her brow creased. Her head had begun to throb again. Amazing how he could give her a headache in just minutes.

The problem with Tair, she thought, was that he was too confident. Too sure of himself, and comfortable with his power.

It didn't help that he was so powerfully shaped, either, as if cut from the desert rock and ravines—solid, invincible. He wasn't just tall, he was broad, strong, big in the way warriors were big. He dwarfed the tent, ate up space with his endless legs and broad shoulders. His wrists and hands were just as immense, his skin a golden-bronze from sun. But it was his hair that gave him the look of the barbarian. His hair was thick, jet-black, and long. His hair ought to be cut or at least tied back from his face but he didn't bother with it, although his jaw was smoother than it had been. Normally it was shadowed with a day's growth of beard but he must have shaved again since morning.

"Tair," she said, and her voice was soft, almost pleading. "I'm not whatever you think I am."

"And what do I think you are?"

"A spy!" Tally flashed, livid all over again.

Tair chuckled softly, dark hair falling forward, shadowing his face. "You object?"

"Of course I'm not a spy. Why would I be a spy? My camera's nice, but it isn't even that high-tech!" She continued to frown at him, hating him, even as she found him horribly, alarmingly attractive. If only she didn't find tall, dark, handsome appealing. If only Paolo had been blonde, frail. But no, Paolo had been her type, too. Brazilian, rugged, muscular, handsome.

But Tair, he put a whole new spin on rugged and muscular.

He put a whole new spin on everything.

"Why do you have such an excellent vocabulary?" she asked, exasperated. It amazed her that at times his English was better than hers. "You speak English flawlessly."

"You pick up things along the way," he answered, shifting a little and then placing one pale suede boot on top of the other. "But tell me more about these first impressions. Why do you think they're wrong?"

He'd changed the subject, she noticed, deliberately focusing the attention away from him back on her. He certainly didn't reveal much about himself and yet there was lots she'd like to know. Like—was he married? Did he have children? How long had he been sheikh? "You want me to divulge all these things about myself but you won't say anything about you."

"I already know me. I don't know you."

"But I don't know you."

"Good. It's better off that way." He grinned, flashing white straight teeth. "How long have you been a photographer?"

She gave up trying to deflect his questioning. At least when talking he wasn't making threats. "About seven years now."

"How did you get into it?"

"I liked photography in high school—worked on the yearbook—but dropped it in college. Then in my early twenties I got a job working in a photo studio at the mall. Lots of family portraits and naked babies lying on sheepskin rugs, but I enjoyed setting up the shots, liked the photography aspect. One thing led to another and here I am."

"In Northern Africa."

She smiled fleetingly. He sounded almost amused and she realized yet again that he wasn't entirely without humor. "Working at the Factoria Mall got boring, as well as claustrophobic. I hated being cooped up inside a big building. I like being outside. Free to roam."

"You had a lot of freedom then as a child?"

Tally suddenly thought of her childhood and her mood instantly changed. She didn't like remembering her childhood, or her home. She didn't want to think about a place that had trapped her, confined her, limiting her opportunities and choices. "No," she answered firmly, and her voice sounded sharper than she intended.

Tally saw his eyebrows lift and she grimaced, gentled her tone. "I was the oldest in a big family. I didn't have a lot of freedom. Just a lot of responsibility."

"So tell me about your family."

But Tally didn't want to talk about her family. Her family had been poor, and poor wasn't interesting or glamorous, but it had taught good lessons. Like, poor tasted hungry. Poor felt weary. Poor smelled fearful. Poor heard despair.

Poor wasn't what Tally wanted to be ever again. Not poor, not helpless, not dependent, not trapped. And maybe she'd never be rich doing her freelance photography, but she always managed to pay her bills and take care of herself.

So no, she didn't like to think about her family or the past, not when it depressed her. Far better to just look forward, set out on fresh adventures, tackle new challenges.

"I was raised in Washington State," she said, deftly side-stepping his question, "between the Cascade Mountains and the Puget Sound. It's rainy and green. No matter where you are you get views of these staggering mountains—Mount Baker, Rainier and St. Helens. The mountains, some extinct volcanoes, are interspersed with lakes and rivers. It's beautiful. Dramatic."

"So why leave it?"

"Because that's where I was raised, but it doesn't feel like my home anymore—"

"Why?" He interrupted, not satisfied with her answer.

"Because."

"Because why?"

She sighed, exasperated. "I need…I want…" She shook her head, irritated by his persistence and her inability to articulate an answer. "Change. I need change."

CHAPTER FIVE

His gaze narrowed, resting on her critically. "But if things were good there?"

Her lips compressed. He was being deliberately provocative. "They weren't, they haven't been good there in years. So I travel. Okay?"

"You still live with your family when you're in Washington?"

"No way." Tally shuddered. "Absolutely not. I have a loft in Seattle. Pioneer Square. It's the historic district. Lots of artists and photographers have galleries there."

"Do you have a gallery?"

"I used to."

"And…?"

"I sold it to come here." She smiled to hide the uneasiness inside of her. Even though she'd begun to find some critical, as well as commercial success as a photographer in downtown Seattle, studio work wasn't her passion. Anyone could stage a scene, get the lighting just right. She needed greater challenges and bigger risks.

Paolo had said she needed the challenges and risks because she was always running away from herself—a statement that had annoyed her tremendously—but there was truth in it. She hadn't been happy at home. She was still trying to understand what happy meant. Happy seemed to be a very hard concept at times.

"I want the memory cards back," she said huskily, looking up, tears in her eyes, blurring her vision. "I want them back, and I know what you've told me, but I don't accept it. There's no way I'll let you keep them or let you delete my work. I've spent weeks in Egypt, Morocco and Baraka photographing children. I'm not about to lose months of work because you disapprove."

She drew a quick breath and reached up to swipe away tears before they could fall. "And if you don't give them to me, when I get out of here, I will tell everyone what you did. I will put it in every magazine, and on every Internet site. I will do endless interviews and send thousands of e-mails. How you kidnapped me, held me hostage, threatened me, intimidated me, took my film—"

"Do you know that our people frown on the use of representational images?"

His quiet question silenced her. He leaned forward, dark gaze intense. "And this problem we have with images extends to photographs. Most of our people have an aversion to cameras, and photographs."

"But no one's had a problem with me taking pictures," she said in a small voice.

"Are you sure? Or have you had to bribe your way into getting the shots you wanted? Money to this person, money to that person?"

Tally swallowed. "My work isn't exploitative—"

"You photograph children and teenagers."

"It's a book about childhood, and the rites and passages of childhood."

"What makes you think you can come here and photograph our children? Families here don't even have photographs of their children. The few photographs we have are formal portraits and those usually commemorate a special occasion."

"I didn't realize. However—" She pushed hair from her face, shoving it behind her ear. "Tair, I understand your resistance to me including the children from the village in my book, but there are nearly three hundred shots on that card. They're not all *your* children and I've spent more than a year on this book. I must finish my book. I need to complete it."

He said nothing. He simply looked at her and the silence grew long, stretching tautly between them.

"Why don't you say anything?" she demanded.

"There's nothing to say."

"But there is. You can tell me when you'll return the cards to me. You can tell me you've changed your mind. You can tell me I'll soon be able to continue my work—"

"But that's not true, so how can I say it?"

"You can't really mean to keep me here!" The threat of tears was real and imminent. Tally closed her eyes, pressed the palms of her hands to her face. All her feelings of good will toward him disappeared. "I don't want this," she protested huskily. "I don't want to be here. I don't want any of this."

"But sometimes what we don't want, is exactly what we need."

"I will keep running away!"

"And I will keep bringing you back."

"Why?"

"Maybe because I want you for me."

Tair's words hit her like ice water thrown in her face. She jerked upright, gasped, blinked, mouth opening and closing in shock and confusion. *He* wanted *her?*

Tair rose slowly, unfolding himself with a deliberate grace and Tally watched him rise, heart in mouth as she realized he was going to reach for her. Her pulse raced, her hands grew damp, her fingers curling into fists even as a strange desire filled her.

She couldn't do this. It was wrong. Everything about it was wrong. "Please go," she choked, voice strangled as she jumped up, taking a panicked step backward. "Please leave now."

But he didn't go. And Tally scooted past him so they circled each other. She was on his side of the table now and she stumbled over one of the cushions he'd been leaning against.

As she kicked aside the cushion, Tally saw a flash of silver and it took her a moment to realize it was a knife. An ornate dagger. His. He must have accidentally dropped it.

The knife wasn't particularly big, the handle jeweled, almost too pretty for a knife, but the blade glinted silver, sharp. She looked at Tair and then down at the knife. It could help her. Save her.

She put her foot on top of the knife, hiding it. It gave her courage. "I don't know what you want from me," she said huskily. "In fact, I don't think you even know what you want from me. Admit you made a mistake and send me back now before it's too late."

"It wasn't a mistake," he answered, arms folding over his chest, eyes narrowing. In the flickering candlelight he looked huge, calm, unflappable.

"But it is. I'm not an object to be caught, trapped, possessed. This isn't my home and I won't live here…although I might die here."

"The way you're going about it, yes, you might. But you could also have a good life here."

"Never." She wouldn't live here, and yes, maybe she would die here, but it was because she had no other choice.

But she wasn't there yet. She still had options. At the very least, she had one option. Fight. Struggle. Survival.

Survival being the only thing important to her at this point.

Veins laced with adrenaline, Tally bent down, grabbed the knife and held it behind her.

"You look so uncomfortable standing there," he said. "Does your arm have a kink in it?"

Hand sweating, she shifted her grip on the dagger's handle. This could go badly, very badly. But she had to try. Had to force the situation somehow. Anything but sit, wait, allow herself to be swamped by despair. Despondency. Passivity.

She'd climbed mountains, scoured the face of granite cliffs. She'd competed in triathlons. Marathons. Could bike, hike, run, sail, surf. If he thought she'd meekly give herself up, hand over her dreams, her goals, her vision for herself—he was wrong. Her eyes burned. Her chest ached. She'd never cut anyone before, never hurt anyone. But she'd hurt him. If she had to.

And she had to.

She had to make him understand she was serious. Had to make him pay attention.

And what if he died?

Her heart did a painful thump, almost as if it were breaking, falling, tumbling into her gut. Well then, she told herself, ignoring the horrible free-fall plummet, he'd die. It's not as though he didn't create this nightmare. This situation was his doing. She was a visitor in his country and he took her, violated her security, stole her security, and now held her captive.

If he had to die, then maybe he had to die.

She swallowed miserably. Hopefully he wouldn't have to die. Hopefully he'd be smart and realize this was going to end badly for both of them.

"No, my arm doesn't have a kink in it," she answered flatly. "I'm armed."

"Armed?" He nearly smiled. "Oh, I see. You found my knife."

So he knew he'd dropped his knife. She brought her arm around, held up the knife, the blade at an angle. Paolo had showed her how to hold a knife, use a knife. He'd taught her the rudiments of weaponry. "Don't move," she warned.

He closed the distance between them, stepping around the table to haul her against him. "Or what?"

Hand shaking, she pressed the tip of the blade to his chest. "I'll kill you," she choked, fire and ice flooding her limbs. "Make one more move and I swear, I'll kill you."

Tair didn't even blink. He simply looked down at her, his expression long suffering. "Put that away."

"No."

"You'll hurt someone."

"Yes. You."

He grabbed her wrist so suddenly she didn't even see him move. But now he held her hand in his and with a swift wrench on her wrist, forced the knife from her hand. Her fingers opened in pain and with a whimper she watched the knife bounce to the carpet.

He let her go and she immediately went to her knees, grabbed the knife and came back at him.

Tair sighed and ripped open his robe. "If you insist," he drawled, now unbuttoning his shirt, "let me at least make this easier for you by giving you the correct target."

The knife in her hand wobbled as she stared at his chest, the bronze skin scarred over dense honed muscle. She looked at the scar tissue that stretched from his sternum toward his left nipple. "Someone's tried this before," she said faintly.

"You're not the first, no." He waited, looked at her. "Give it a shot. The skin's tough but you might be able to do it."

Tally couldn't look away from the thick scarring, the seams marring his beautiful skin. Fresh tears filled her eyes and with a groan of despair she gave him the knife. "Go," she said. "Just go. Get out of here."

Tair had played it cool in the her tent, but once he'd left his temper surged and he yanked off his robe and tugged on the shirt, freeing it from his trousers and then opening it to the chest, letting the night air cool his skin.

Savage, that's how he felt tonight. A savage on fire. A savage burning from the inside out.

Standing at the edge of camp, facing the endless desert illuminated only by the moon overhead, Tair could see the sandstorm from earlier, and then the sky once they'd returned, the sky seemed to bleed tonight as the sun set, orange weeping into red against bruised violet. He'd seen the sandstorm on the horizon. He'd seen the clouds gather, the dark brown turning black as the storm touched down, wreaking havoc with the wild whipping winds that decimated everything in its path.

He hadn't thought he'd reach the woman in time.

He hadn't thought he'd save her.

He blew out a breath, the air a harsh exhale. He'd told his men to turn back. Told them to return to camp and safety and he alone went ahead for her.

He wasn't afraid to die. He knew he'd die eventually, it was just a matter of time, but he feared for her. She wasn't of his people, didn't know the desert as he did. She would have suffered alone and he couldn't allow that. If she were to perish he should at least be there with her. No woman should die afraid and alone. It was wrong. Went against every belief he had, every conviction he held.

No, the American didn't understand his world. His world was primitive and it fit him. Here justice—and death—came swiftly. In the desert, justice was meted out by a fierce and unwavering hand. If not nature's, then his.

After all, this was his country, his people, his land, his desert, his sun. His father had ruled before him and his father before that, and back it went, on and on, generation after generation.

Tair knew what the American woman said, knew in her world what he did was criminal, knew in her world he had no right. But she wasn't in her world, she was in his, and here what he did was allowed. Permissible. Just.

She'd get used to his world. Sooner or later.

Tally couldn't sleep that night. Every time she drifted off, some thought, some terror brought her back awake again.

The fact that she found Tair attractive—in any size, shape or form—horrified her. He wasn't a good man, nor kind, nor gentle, nor sophisticated. He might have the title of sheikh, but underneath it all he was a kidnapper, a bully and a thief. But knowing that, accepting that, she still couldn't hurt him.

This is why she couldn't stay. This is why she had to go. She was losing her mind, losing perspective. She couldn't allow a desert barbarian to confuse her. And she was confused. Very.

Just before dawn, Tally left her bed. She'd leave while everyone still slept. She'd go on foot, but she'd take the dried fruit she'd been saving from her meals, and the dried bread, and the jug of water from her bedside chest and go before camp woke.

The sun was just breaking on the horizon when she left her tent. The camp's three-legged dog stirred from his place by the now cold fire and bounded toward her. Before he could bark, Tally broke off a piece of bread, tossed it at him, and the mutt, pouncing on the bread, was quite happy to eat not bark, allowing Tally to leave camp undisturbed.

"She's left, sir. Again." It was Tair's elderly Berber servant standing at the entrance of Tair's tent, his head bowed.

"I'm sorry," the servant added apologetically, his head drooping even lower in disgrace. "She must have left early, when the camp was still sleeping."

Tair briefly closed his eyes and pressed two fingers to the bridge of his nose. "Footprints?"

"Yes. West, toward the wadi, sir."

Tair bit back his oath of impatience and irritation. This Tally was proving to be a great deal of trouble for just one woman. "Thank you," he said, remaining at his desk where he'd been drafting a document that would eventually be sent to the royal palace in Atiq, to the attention of Malik Nuri, the Sultan of Baraka.

The servant hesitated. "Do you want me to send someone after her?"

"No."

And the elderly man hesitated even longer—a testament to his inherent goodness. "It wouldn't be any trouble. We have men to spare at the moment—"

"Not necessary. But thank you." Tair didn't even look up.

His man murmured acknowledgment and exited, letting the tent flap fall behind him and it wasn't until Tair was alone that he glanced up, forehead furrowing with aggravation.

Tally lacked sense even a child would have. Rushing blindly into the desert. Running off with no chance of escape. She must have a death wish. She had to know she couldn't—wouldn't—survive even twenty-four hours in the desert unprotected.

Sighing, he leaned back in his chair and stared across the tent to the cushions scattered on the floor.

The whole point of kidnapping a woman and making her yours was that one had effectively bypassed pretense and any ridiculous notions of romance.

Tair didn't do romance. He didn't woo or court. He didn't have time, and even if he did, he wouldn't anyway. Wooing was for men who lacked confidence in their ability to make a woman adapt, conform, behave. And that had never been Tair's problem. Women—for better or worse—liked him. Loved him. He didn't always love back but that was his fault. He didn't love, didn't know how to love, not the way women wanted to be loved and yet he'd accepted this flaw in his personality, realizing he had strengths that compensated for his deficiencies.

He was loyal. He was strong. He understood and respected commitment.

He was also wealthy enough, and although scarred—he'd fought in just one too many battles—he wasn't completely deformed and women so far hadn't minded the wounds. In fact, women—who would ever understand them?—seemed to like the scars. Made them protective.

Tair snorted to himself. Women made no sense but that was nothing new.

Maybe he'd just have to tie Tally up. She'd hate it but maybe that's what he needed to do. Tie her to the pole in the center of his tent, keep her tethered like one of the baby goats that tended to wander off if not kept safely roped.

And then picking up his pen, Tair returned to his work, determined to finish his letter before setting off in search of the woman he had decided would be his. Even if she hadn't accepted it yet.

So this was how she was going to die. An awful, horrible death. Suffocation by sand.

Tally had always feared drowning in the ocean but this would be just as bad. Sliding beneath the surface, buried in a sea of sand. Sand in her eyes, her nose, her mouth. Sand filling her lungs.

Tortured by the thought, Tally struggled, grappling upward but the movement worked against her and she dropped lower, sliding down instead of up. She'd heard that fighting quicksand was a death sentence, but this wasn't real quicksand, was it? She'd never heard of desert quicksand but one moment she'd been walking and the next the world beneath her gave away.

Shock caused her to kick her legs and down she went lower, the sand completely enclosing the lower half of her body. She'd slipped further down in the hour she'd been trapped.

Don't panic, she told herself, even as she flailed again, and the flailing just pulled her down deeper, faster.

Come on, Tal, get control. This won't be pleasant. No need to rush blindly into this. Try at least to savor your last hour of life.

The realization that she was trapped and unable to free herself finally hit home and some of the desperate fight left her. No reason to hurry death along. And she wasn't sinking anymore. For a moment she just rested there, ribs buried, legs gone, but her arms were still free and she could breathe. That was something.

A big something.

Now all she had to do was stay relaxed and think.

Think.

There's got to be a way out.

But turning her head, she could see nothing to grab, nothing secure to hold. No way to pull herself out.

She drew a deep breath and felt the sand give and she slipped, not far, just a couple inches, but that was far enough.

To die in quicksand.

No one died in quicksand. People couldn't die in quicksand. And desert quicksand? Didn't exist. That was just movie stuff.

And yet she was trapped and it was sand.

Tally felt the slow slip of sand and knew she was sinking again, still slowly, steadily, sliding though to where? What lay beneath the sand? A hole? More ground? A cave? Why had the sand beneath her given way?

Tally shuddered imagining the very end and her shudder speeded the slipping sand. Or maybe it was her weight—and gravity—pulling her faster now but she continued to drop, lower, much lower, the weight of the sand on her chest, pressing hot and hard against her lungs.

Her pulse quickened and adrenaline coursed through her. Hell, hell, hell.

She didn't want to go this way. Didn't want to go at all, but certainly not this way. And the more she knew she didn't want to suffocate in sand, the harder she thrashed the lower she slipped.

God, don't let me die this way!

"Stop fighting," a familiar voice said from behind her.

"Tair?" Hot tears surged to her eyes. Relief flooded through her. She tried to turn to see him and just sank deeper.

"You've got to stop moving," he said, walking around the side of the sandpit, keeping a careful distance between them.

The sand was up to her armpits and weighing heavy on her chest. "Can you get me out?"

"Yes. After we talk."

Tally instinctively kicked, feeling the sand creep through the armholes of her shirt, sliding against her bare skin. "Talk now? Tair, I can hardly breathe!"

"Then don't talk, listen to me." He crouched down, arms resting on his knees, white robe billowing. "I'm losing patience, Tally. This is the second day in a row I've had to save your skin and it's getting old."

"You're giving me a lecture now?"

"You're making life harder for everyone. You need to accept your fate more gracefully—"

"Accept being kidnapped?" Her voice rose in an indignant howl. "No. Never! This is not my fate. My fate isn't to be trapped in the desert forever with you."

"You're right," he answered mildly. "It seems your fate is to die today in quicksand."

"Tair!"

"It's one or the other, Woman. Make up your mind. I haven't all day." He leaned back, took a seat on the sand. "Actually, you haven't all day. But why beat the point to death? It's your life, not mine."

"Stop threatening me and just get me out."

"Tsk tsk," he chided her. "So rude. Is that the way to ask for help?"

"You know I want your help."

"You don't appreciate all the things I do for you."

"Do for me?" Her voice rose as she slipped lower, sand engulfing her all the way to her shoulders. "Tair, I'm going to go under. Get me out now."

"Ask nicely."

"This is a game to you!"

"I wouldn't call it a game, but it is interesting. Will the American ask for help or will she sink all the way under?"

"Tair."

"Ask for help, Tally."

She felt wild, panicked. "You're not being fair."

"Life's not fair." His dark gaze met hers and held. "Learn to ask for help, Tally."

"I did. I asked you to get me out."

"It wasn't very polite."

She could feel the sand on her neck, feel it press relentlessly, feel the slippery cool grains everywhere and her head spun, dizzy. "I hate you."

He sighed. "Why are you so stubborn?"

"Why are you?" Tears filled her eyes and she couldn't even brush them away. "You know I can't get out of here without your help but you're making me beg and that's cruel—"

"Refusing to ask for help is worse. That's a death wish, and stupid."

"What word do you want? What is it you want to hear? Tair, you're so marvelous. Or Tair, you're my man. What is it you want?"

The edge of his mouth tugged. "That's quite gratifying, Woman, but I was actually just looking for please."

Tair rose in one fluid motion, white robes swirling and going to his horse, he withdrew a rope, tied it to his stallion's saddle and returned to her side.

He stretched out on the sand, and inched his way toward her and tossed the looped rope around her shoulders, and tugged, the loop tightened lasso-like and he had her secure.

Whistling to his horse, the stallion began to back up and with Tair guiding the rope, he managed to drag Tally free of the sand.

"Thank you," Tally choked, tears streaming and she rubbed one cheek and then the other, her face streaked with tears and sand.

"You're welcome." He whistled again to the stallion and the horse trotted over. Swinging into his saddle, he leaned down, held an arm out to Tally. "Let's go home."

Tally froze. She didn't put her hand in his. "But that's the problem, Tair. It's not my home."

"Here we go again," he muttered beneath his breath.

"It's not."

"I don't want to do this now. The sand is still unstable from yesterday's storm. There are probably more sand traps out here. If you really want me to leave you here, fine. But I'm going home."

Tally sagged, exhausted, forlorn. "I don't want to be left here."

"Then you're accepting my protection?"

Fresh tears burned her eyes but she wouldn't let them fall. "No." She turned, stared out across the desert that had become a treacherous prison and she wondered when and how this would end. Worn out, worn down she couldn't keep running away but how to give up her world? Her life? Her dreams? Because she knew once she said yes, there would be no going back.

Tair swore softly and with a scoop of his arm lifted Tally up, settling her in his saddle in front of him. His arm was hard around her, holding her completely immobile. "This is getting familiar," he said, dragging her even closer.

Tally shivered at the feel of his chest against her back, his body hard, solid, warm.

It wasn't a particularly long ride back to camp and as they arrived, Tair's men looked away, their heads turned, gazes respectfully fixed elsewhere as Tair wrestled with what they must think a truly demented woman. Well let them think she was mad. Because she wasn't going to go back without a fight. She wasn't going to just accept whatever sentence Tair handed out.

They were back. The men spilled from his camp, watching as Tair reined his horse to a stop but none actually looked at her.

Not a good sign, Tally thought, defensively. "You can't keep me here," she whispered. "I will take off first chance I can. I will continue to go—"

"You've nearly died in a sandstorm, spent a frightening afternoon in a sandpit. What do you want to happen now?"

"I don't know, but I'm beginning to think being eaten by a snake is preferable to staying here with you."

"Now come," Tair said, sliding off the horse and yanking her down behind him, "that's unfair. You haven't even been bedded by me yet. You might actually like being my woman."

"Never."

He clucked disapprovingly, and walked toward his tent, strides long, determined, his hold on her wrist just as hard. "The least you could do is withhold judgment until I've had you."

He tossed aside the curtainlike flap and pulled her inside. The flap snapped closed. "Which I intend to do—" he broke off as his gaze swept over her, up and down "—as soon as you bathe. You, my dear woman, reek."

"Reek?" Her voice rose and yet she threw her shoulders back, puffed her chest out. "Well, that's just lovely considering you've kept me in rank tents, eating tough goat meat and drinking warm goat's milk for days. You've no proper bath, no shampoo, no lotions, no scented oils. Nothing. I thought sheikhs lived in beautiful palaces filled with sunken tiled baths and gorgeous mosaic arches. But no. I have to get kidnapped by a sheikh who lives like a peasant with nothing but a half dozen ancient tents to his name."

Tair's jaw jutted. "You've forgotten my horse."

"I have." Her chest rose and fell with each rapid breath. "But one horse doesn't make a kingdom, Sheikh al Tayer—"

"It's el-Tayer. You're in Northern Africa not the Middle East."

She gestured impatiently. "The point is, where's Aladdin when you need him? Where's my genie to make everything beautiful? Because you might be a sheikh, *el-Tayer,* but this isn't my fantasy. Not even close."

"Enough," Tair ground out, dragging her toward him. "This may not be your idea of paradise, but I've had it with the running away, and pulling knives, and putting your life in danger. It's stopping. Now. Understand me?"

But he didn't give her a chance to answer. Instead he pulled her into his arms, fitting her against his body so that her softness curved against his hardness, her hips cradling his, her thighs caught between his own, her breasts crushed to his chest.

Heat flared in her cheeks, heat and awareness as well as shame. She wanted him, wanted this contact with him and yet everything about him was lethal, destructive. "Let me go," she begged.

His hand wound through her hair, forming a rope of the thick brown strands. "No."

She tried to push away from him but couldn't, not when he held her so securely. His head lowered, and fire flashed in his dark eyes. She felt her knees start to buckle as she realized that he was going to kiss her—whether she wanted him to or not.

His mouth covered hers hard, a fierce kiss of possession. She stiffened at the touch of his mouth on hers, stiffened from shock as well as pleasure. His lips made her own mouth feel hot, sensitive, alive and she shivered as his lips moved over hers, drawing a response.

He was warm and his beard rough and yet his lips were cool, firm, teasing. They teased her now and her lips parted beneath his, allowing him in and she arched helplessly against his heat, her lower body tingling as desire coiled in her belly, tight and hungry.

She wanted him. Oh God she wanted him and yet going to bed—making love—wasn't an option. She had to know that. She had to be smart enough to know she couldn't ever give herself to this man. And even knowing that, she couldn't end the kiss, couldn't break free.

It was Tair who finally lifted his head, his hands slipping from her hair to frame her face. "Tell me, when is this foolish, dangerous behavior going to end?"

CHAPTER SIX

TALLY could barely draw a breath, her heart pounding fast and furious, her pulse unsteady.

She heard his question but couldn't speak, not when her brain was too busy analyzing everything happening. Like the way he held her face, and the way his fingers curved to fit her jawbone and the almost tender way he plucked a hair from her eye and smoothed it back from her face.

She fought to steady her breathing.

"This must stop," he continued. "You're putting not just your life at risk, but mine as well as my men."

"Then let me go."

"That's not an option—"

"Why not?"

"Because you're mine now," he answered simply.

Tair's answer cut through her haze of emotion and sensation. She pushed his hands away and took one step back, and then another. She was his.

He said she was his...

She'd never been anyone's. Not even Paolo's, not even when she gave her body to him. Paolo hadn't been the marrying kind and she knew there'd be no settling down with him, no house, no children, nothing like that.

But Tair. Tair. He was so different. He was so strong, so intense, so possessive. From the moment he'd hauled her onto his horse he'd acted as though she were his and there were times it infuriated her and then times it did something to her, touched her, undid her.

She hadn't really felt like anyone's in so long.

Tally put a hand to her temple, tried to clear her head. "I'll keep running away, Tair."

"And go where, Woman?" He rarely raised his voice but it was loud now. "You're in the middle of the Sahara Desert. Doesn't that mean anything? Or maybe you truly have a death wish, and if that's the case, tell me now and I'll stop rushing after you."

All fuzziness in her head disappeared, all tenderness and ambivalence vanishing in the face of his insensitivity and arrogance. "Rushing?" she spluttered. *"Rushing?* I wouldn't say you rush. It seems to me you enjoy waiting until the last possible moment to do the big rescue."

"I can't drop everything every time you decide it's time to run away again."

"Drop *everything?* Sheikh Tair, forgive me, but no one here does anything but drink tea and play dice."

"It's not dice and we don't just drink tea. My men all have specific jobs they do."

"That's right. They have guns to clean." She clapped a hand to her forehead. "Silly me. How could I forget?"

"Every time I set off, my men accompanied me until I sent them back. Every time I left camp to look for you we took risks and if you don't appreciate me, you better damn well appreciate my men."

Tears filled her eyes and furiously she rubbed them away. "You keep acting as though I should be grateful you kidnapped me from the medina. But I didn't ask to have my life turned upside down. I didn't ask for any of this, not even your protection!"

"But that's not true. You came to our world, we didn't go to yours."

And that, Tally thought, shoulders slumping, was a most excellent point.

She walked away from him, a fist pressed to her mouth as she realized for the first time how this all must seem to him. He wasn't Western, he wasn't anything like the men in her world, and the rules here were so different. If as he said, she was traveling with dangerous men, he'd done what he'd thought was right, behaved fairly, protectively.

She focused on one of the wool pillows lying on the low bed. It was a beautiful pattern, handwoven. "How could you leave me in the quicksand so long?" Her voice broke and a lump filled her throat. "I could have died."

Tair didn't immediately answer and she closed her eyes as the silence stretched. Then she felt his hand touch her back, his palm warm, firm.

"Is that what this is really about?" he asked. "That I made you ask for help?"

She wiped away one tear and then another. "Maybe."

He put his hands on her shoulders and slowly turned her around. "All you had to do was ask for help. It was your impulsiveness that got you into trouble in the first place. You ran off. You were just lucky I decided to go search for you."

Lucky, huh? Tally sniffed. "If I'd been lucky I wouldn't have been in the medina when you were. If I were lucky you would have kidnapped some other poor Western woman. That's my definition of luck."

He shrugged, but in his eyes was a glimmer of a smile. "Perhaps it's a cultural difference, but to be given the gift of life—not just once, but twice—that's good fortune."

"You're speaking of the two times you saved me."

"Three now."

She stared up into his hard, arrogant features. Big nose, dark eyes, fierce mouth. And strangely—beautiful. God, she hated him. And wanted him. And hated herself for still finding him so attractive, despite everything that had taken place between them. "I don't know that you saved me three times," she answered, striving to sound cool. "The first time you'd almost killed me so I don't know if that counts."

The corners of his mouth tugged. "To show you I am a fair man, I am willing to compromise and will agree that according to your definition, I've only saved your life twice."

Tally hid her own reluctant smile, cleared her throat. "Since we're trying to be accurate, I think it should be mentioned that your rescue today would have been more heroic if you hadn't waited until I nearly slid all the way under."

He sighed and yet the heavy sigh was contradicted by the warmth in his eyes. "I've never met a woman that demands so much and expresses so little gratitude."

"We're talking about my life, Sheikh Tair!"

"Then ask for help, Woman. Don't wait until the grains of sand fill your nose. Ask for help while you still have air to speak with."

And then his head dropped and he covered her mouth with his once again, his lips coaxing and she didn't need much encouragement. Her mouth loved the feel of his, her body wanted him and her arms slid up around his neck as she kissed him back.

They were interrupted by a shout outside the tent, the voice raised in alarm.

Tair pulled away and turned to leave but not before he pressed a swift kiss to her brow. "I shall return for dinner. Wait for me."

Tally watched from her tent as men gathered around Tair in the deepening twilight. He was gesturing, speaking, giving orders. Some men began to saddle up while others packed bags. They were going somewhere and they had guns.

She felt her stomach flip and fall and she grabbed at the tent, held on. She wanted to rush out, confront Tair, ask what was happening but didn't dare, not after the day they'd just had.

Instead she stood in the shadows and watched as Tair,

leading twenty-some men, set off on their horses at a full speed gallop.

Tally had taken a bath, dressed in the simple black robe that Tair's elderly servant supplied, and with candles lit in her tent, tried to pass the time until Tair returned but he was gone a long time and the hours passed slowly.

Her stomach growled late in the night and finally the elderly Berber brought her food and even though she was hungry, Tally refused. "I'm waiting for Tair," she said to the old man.

"Ash?" he asked. What?

"I'm waiting for Tair."

The old man stared at her uncomprehendingly.

"Tair," Tally repeated and this time she stood on her toes, lifted her hand high above her head to indicate Tair's immense height. *"Tair."*

The elderly man only looked more puzzled and Tally wanted to pull her hair out in mad chunks. This was a nightmare. A nightmare. How could Tair think she could possibly stay here, the only woman—and a Western woman at that— in this camp? He was out of his mind.

"Tair," Tally said more loudly.

The old man just looked at her with absolute incomprehension.

"He doesn't have a clue as to what you're saying," an amused voice said behind her and Tally spun around.

"How long have you been standing there?" she demanded, exhaling a huffy puff even as she pushed her long hair back from her face.

"Long enough to enjoy your pantomime."

"Very funny." But it was, she knew and she smiled reluctantly. "So you're back. Did you get the bad guys?"

His lips curved but the smile didn't touch his eyes. "Most of them."

She felt his mood then and it was somber, heavy, and Tally

wondered just what had taken place out there in the desert to-night. "Hungry?" she asked more gently.

He nodded. "Let me just wash. I'll be right back." He returned shortly, jaw clean shaven, his hair wet, combed back from his face, the thick shoulder-length strands a glossy black in the soft yellow candlelight.

"You look…nice," Tally said awkwardly, shyly.

Tair laughed. "You sound so surprised."

"No, I…um, no." Blushing she moved to the table laden with trays and bowls, more food than Tally had seen in a long time. "No," she repeated and knelt on one side of the table. "Let's eat."

Over dinner she asked him why the older man didn't understand her when she asked for him.

"No one here knows me as Tair," he answered, dipping a hunk of the bread in the stew.

"Then what do they call you?"

"Sheikh Zein el-Tayer. Or Soussi al-Kebir."

Chief of the Soussi Desert. Tally bit her lip, thinking how odd it was that his name which had been so strange was now so familiar. "How does Tair come from Tayer?"

He grimaced. "Good question. It's pronounced like the English word for tire, and it shouldn't be hard to say but when I attended boarding school in England, the headmaster could never say my name quite right and pretty soon all the boys were calling me Tair."

"An English boarding school? That explains some things. So, did it bother you they couldn't get your name right?"

"No. A name's a name. There are other things more pressing."

"Like?"

"Politics. Survival." He hesitated and when Tally said nothing he continued. "You don't know our history, or our culture so I can't expect you to understand the turmoil in this region, but politics have given us a violent legacy. We've fought to maintain our independence but it's not been without great personal cost."

She didn't know if it was his expression, or his tone, but she knew somehow, sensed it maybe, that he'd suffered. Personally suffered. It wasn't just his people's conflict but his own. "Those scars," she said hesitantly, indicating his torso where his robe covered the thickened tissue crisscrossing his chest, "are they a result of this violent legacy?"

"Yes."

She looked at him closely, really looked at him and she saw lines in his face, creases at his eyes, grooves near his mouth and the hollows beneath his high cheekbones. "You've been to war?"

"I live the war."

She didn't know what that meant. It was such a vague, cryptic thing to say. Part of her wanted to know what he meant and another part of her didn't. He was frightening, too frightening, his body a canvas of cuts and wounds, his strength formidable, his courage incomparable. She'd never met anyone who could do what he could do. She'd never thought it possible that a man could do what Tair did.

But there was a dark side, too. He wasn't a good man, couldn't by any stretch of the imagination be called thoughtful, kind, or compassionate. "How do you live war?"

"You attack. Steal. Injure. Kill."

"I see." And she did, too well. She could picture him doing all of the above, and remorselessly, as well. "You've killed in self-defense?"

"If you want to call it that."

Again she hesitated. "And if I don't?"

"It's what it is."

He met her questioning look with a slow, mocking smile. "Revenge," he added quietly. "A settling of scores."

"Revenge for what?"

"Taking what was mine."

"Yours as in money…land…?"

"As in women and children."

Tally swallowed, put down her bread and dusted her fingers off. "You've been married?"

"Yes."

She didn't know what to say next. For some reason she couldn't bring herself to ask about his wife. She knew men in Baraka and Ouaha often had several wives but Tally didn't want to imagine Tair with wives, couldn't stand to think he had another woman somewhere, one that belonged to him legally, morally.

She shifted uncomfortably, appetite gone. Happiness fading.

"What's wrong?" he asked, watching her.

Tally shook her head. It would be too ridiculous to tell him.

"Did I ever tell you that my father kidnapped my mother?" Tair asked conversationally, before taking another bite.

She looked up, brows pulling. "No."

"Mmmm." He swallowed, took a drink from his cup. "You asked me before why my English was so good and it's because my mother was English. She was a schoolteacher. She was teaching for the International School in Atiq when my father saw her, kidnapped her, took her to his kasbah and made her his."

"Did your mother hate your father for what he did?"

Tair's mouth quirked. "No. She loved him. They were still quite together when my father died." He turned his cup on the table, ran his finger over the glazed pottery. "My mother never returned to Britain. She stayed here in Ouaha and then only recently has moved to Baraka. She has a home in Atiq." He half smiled. "She's in her sixties and she's teaching again."

"Your mother has gone back to work?" Tally was torn between admiration and concern.

"She wanted to. She loved teaching and she missed my father and my brothers. Atiq's a better place for her now." He broke off another hunk of bread. "You'll have to meet her. She's almost as feisty as you."

Tally heard the warmth in his voice and looking up, her eyes met his. The expression in his eyes was nearly as warm as his voice.

Her heart beat double-time. Butterflies filled her middle. She remembered the kiss from earlier. Remembered the feel of his mouth and his hands on her skin.

Still half smiling, Tair asked, "Your father didn't kidnap your mother?"

Tally's mind flashed to the cramped trailer, and the trailer park, she'd grown up in and cringed inwardly. He might as well have, she thought, thinking about her father who couldn't ever keep a job thanks to his drinking and her mother who juggled several but never particularly well. Her past seemed to be a horrible lesson in mediocrity. Everything she'd learned had been, don't do this if you want to succeed. "No. No kidnapping involved."

She felt his dark gaze move leisurely across her features, studying, analyzing.

"There's that expression again," he said. "You get that look every time you talk about your family. It's so hard, so judgmental. I thought perhaps the first time it was my imagination but you do it every time you speak of them. That look of disappointment. Disapproval."

She felt the muscles pull in her jaw, the jaw itself flexing and he was right. There was no point in contradicting him. "My life hasn't been like yours," she finally said when the silence dragged too long. Tair wasn't very good at filling silences and while she wasn't particularly fond of chatter, she'd rather talk than sit awkwardly silent with Tair watching her.

And he did watch her. He watched her always, watched her with intense speculation. A snake in the desert. A hawk in the sky. He was simply biding his time. Waiting.

Waiting.

Tally ground her teeth, tension making her shoulders, head, jaw ache. "I wasn't raised with money. We didn't have any.

We didn't even go to college. At least, not away, not to the good ones, the expensive ones. My younger sister, Mandy, got an athletic scholarship to Washington State University and one of my brothers went to University of Washington while another went to school in California—but that's because they played sports. I didn't."

"So what did you do?"

She looked at him from beneath her eyelashes, her teeth clicking as she bit down once and again. Goddamn him. She hated his stupid questions. Stupid annoying questions. Stupid annoying facts. He was a sheikh and she was a poor church mouse.

From a trailer park.

From North Bend.

From a place that got more rain and cloud than sun.

She sighed, rubbed her neck, stretched a little. Her head hurt, filled with strange pain and she'd thought it was tension, but wasn't so sure anymore. "I went to Bellevue City College." She swallowed, her mouth suddenly dry, her tongue feeling thick, numb at the tip. "Took courses there and then went to work."

"I've heard of Bellevue. Home of Microsoft, and Bill Gates, yes?"

"More or less." She closed her eyes, woozy. Tally drew a deep breath and then another. Maybe it was just remembering the past that made her nauseous. Maybe it was the hurt that lingered all these years later.

Why tell him the truth about her past? Why did he need to know her real world? There was no reason he should have all the details.

She swallowed with difficulty, her throat thickening. Wouldn't it be better to just pretend she was someone she wasn't? Wouldn't it make more sense to go with the rich and fashionably chic world of Bellevue instead of the damp misty town at the base of the Cascade mountain range? Pretend she shopped at Bellevue Square instead of North Bend's outlet stores? Pretend she had money to spend in the first place...?

"You didn't play sports?" Tair asked, persisting with his line of questioning.

His voice seemed to come from far away. She looked at him, forced herself to focus. "No. Not really." Her forehead furrowed as she looked at a spot on the low table between them. "Well, I did, in high school. Volleyball." She suddenly smiled, a wry remembrance. She'd been good, too. Really good. Not the tallest, but dang, she'd been fast, and aggressive. Tally had gone after every ball...

"I used to love volleyball. And softball. But volleyball was my sport." Her head cocked and she seemed to be looking back, listening to voices in the past and her smile faded. "I used to spend hours working with my sister Mandy." She hesitated, choosing her words more slowly. "I was glad Mandy got the scholarship. Mandy was good. At least one of us got a chance to go to college. Play in college, and not just any school, but a good school. A big name school.

Tair's dark eyes rested on her face, his expression perfectly blank. "But you were good, too."

Tally briefly nodded. She nearly smiled but it was too much effort. "Yes."

"Why didn't you get a scholarship then?"

She looked off to the side again, looking back to a past that had been more pain than pleasure. "I was the oldest."

"And?"

"Needed at home."

Tair's black eyebrows pulled. "So you were awarded a scholarship?"

To UCLA. A great school with a great program. And she couldn't go, couldn't take it. "My parents—" She broke off, swallowed, shoulders shifting in that same uneasy shrug. If only she felt better. If only her head didn't hurt so. "Dad—" She broke off, tried again, "Dad wasn't well and Mom was working full-time. Someone had to watch the younger ones."

"And that someone was you."

It took Tally a long moment to speak. "The oldest."

"And a girl."

Her tight, pained smile grew even tighter, more painful. "I guess being a girl has its drawbacks in every culture."

So that was it, Tair thought, leaning back, absorbing the revelation. This wasn't just about him and her—this was bigger, greater. This was about gender. Identity. Discrimination.

Tally leaned forward against the table. She felt increasingly woozy and weak.

Something was wrong.

Her head swam and her stomach cramped. Her insides felt as though boiling oil had been poured through her. Pain filled her, wrenching her insides, surging through her veins. She nearly crumpled forward, her hand knocking her bowl aside.

"Woman," Tair said.

She could barely focus, unable to get beyond the fire twisting her insides into two. But his voice was strong, commanding.

Tally looked at Tair, stricken, bewildered. Something was very wrong. Something she'd eaten. Drunk.

"Tally?"

There were two of him. Now three. She blinked, eyes heavy, hot with pain, the same fire consuming her belly. "What have you done?" she choked, before slipping sideways to the floor.

OFFICIAL OPINION POLL

ANSWER 3 QUESTIONS AND WE'LL SEND YOU
2 FREE BOOKS AND A FREE GIFT!

0074823 |||||||||||| |||||||| |||||||| FREE GIFT CLAIM # 3953

YOUR OPINION COUNTS!

Please check TRUE or FALSE below to express your opinion about the following statements:

Q1 Do you believe in "true love"?

"TRUE LOVE HAPPENS ONLY ONCE IN A LIFETIME."
○ TRUE
○ FALSE

Q2 Do you think marriage has any value in today's world?

"YOU CAN BE TOTALLY COMMITTED TO SOMEONE WITHOUT BEING MARRIED."
○ TRUE
○ FALSE

Q3 What kind of books do you enjoy?

"A GREAT NOVEL MUST HAVE A HAPPY ENDING."
○ TRUE
○ FALSE

YES, I have scratched the area below.

Please send me the 2 **FREE BOOKS** and **FREE GIFT** for which I qualify. I understand I am under no obligation to purchase any books, as explained on the back of this card.

306 HDL EFV7   106 HDL EFUW

FIRST NAME	LAST NAME

ADDRESS

APT.#	CITY

STATE/PROV.	ZIP/POSTAL CODE

www.eHarlequin.com

(HTF-P-06/06)

DETACH AND MAIL CARD TODAY!

The Harlequin Reader Service® — Here's how it works:

Accepting your 2 free books and mystery gift places you under no obligation to buy anything. You may keep the books and gift and return the shipping statement marked "cancel." If you do not cancel, about a month later we'll send you 6 additional books and bill you just $3.80 each in the U.S., or $4.47 each in Canada, plus 25¢ shipping & handling per book and applicable taxes if any.* That's the complete price and – compared to cover prices of $4.50 each in the U.S., and $5.25 each in Canada – it's quite a bargain! You may cancel at any time, but if you choose to continue, every month we'll send you 6 more books which you may either purchase at the discount price or return to us and cancel your subscription.

*Terms and prices subject to change without notice. Sales tax applicable in N.Y. Canadian residents will be charged applicable provincial taxes and GST.

If offer card is missing write to: The Harlequin Reader Service, 3010 Walden Ave., P.O. Box 1867, Buffalo, NY 14240-1867

NO POSTAGE
NECESSARY
IF MAILED
IN THE
UNITED STATES

BUSINESS REPLY MAIL
FIRST-CLASS MAIL   PERMIT NO. 717-003   BUFFALO, NY

POSTAGE WILL BE PAID BY ADDRESSEE

HARLEQUIN READER SERVICE
3010 WALDEN AVE
PO BOX 1867
BUFFALO NY 14240-9952

CHAPTER SEVEN

TAIR didn't waste any time sending for a doctor. This wasn't ordinary food poisoning. It was deliberate, and whatever had been slipped into Tally's food—or drink—could be fatal, toxic.

Tair did what he could until the doctor arrived. He followed the simple universal antidote his mother had used with them: two parts wood charcoal, one part magnesia milk and one part of very strong tea. He gave her two tablespoons of the mixture in a little bit of water. He didn't know what she'd ingested, but knew that if the poison was metallic or alkaline, the tannic acid in the tea would neutralize it. If the poison was acid, the magnesia would neutralize it. And the wood charcoal even in a very little dose can absorb strong quantities of toxin.

With his servant's help, he got the antidote in her, before inducing vomiting. After she'd thrown up, he gave her another dose of the antidote and then pumped as many liquids as he could get down her throat—not an easy feat considering she was oblivious to everything except the nightmare of pain that had swallowed her whole.

Even as he fought to save her, he pieced together the situation, needing to know who, what, where, how as quickly as he could. This wasn't an accident. Someone had deliberately doctored her food and drink. But which of his men would do it, and why?

The doctor arrived at dawn, less than seven hours after

Tally had been poisoned, arriving precisely the same time Tair discovered it was Ashraf who committed the crime.

Tair had Ashraf isolated and monitored but Tair couldn't deal personally with him until after the doctor had seen Tally.

"The Devil's Herb," the doctor said, naming the toxic herb he suspected she'd ingested after checking her pulse, her eyes, and her tongue, as he prepared an injection.

Tair lifted the glass vial, checking the medicine the doctor was about to administer.

"It's the fastest, best antidote for the central toxic effects."

Tair nodded, still studying the bottle. The Devil's Herb—belladonna—was extremely toxic, often fatal, death usually resulting from asphyxiation but the universal antidote seemed to have helped Tally. Now he just wanted to know she'd be okay.

"She'll be sick for quite a while," the doctor concluded, finishing administering the injection. "You'll find that she's restless, agitated. She'll experience varying degrees of hallucinations, delirium, tremors, but she should get through."

Should, Tair silently repeated, leaving Tally in the doctor's care while he went to deal with Ashraf.

Tair gave Ashraf an opportunity to explain what he'd done and why, and Ashraf was all too happy to talk and Tair listened to Ashraf without interrupting him.

This was about *sehour,* Ashraf said, witchcraft. Tair hid his disgust as Ashraf talked. He couldn't believe it. Not just poison, but witchcraft. His people were superstitious. But Ashraf was not at all repentant.

"I did not give her poison," Ashraf said. "It's a *potion,* a potion to drive her and the evil eye away. She will bring destruction on all of us if we don't. She must go."

"What have you been smoking?" Tair demanded shortly, stunned that it was Ashraf who had done this. Ashraf had served him well for years.

"She's not Aisha Qandisha," Tair added, referring to the

mythical figure many of the people in the countryside believed existed.

Aisha Qandisha was reportedly a beautiful, seductive woman with the legs of a goat and she lived in riverbeds, in flames, and sandstorms. She is said to appear to men in dreams, enchanting them, enslaving them and children always fear her but Tally wasn't a mythical figure, and he'd seen her legs—and they were far from goatlike.

But Ashraf had his own ideas and shook his head. "The sehirra gave me something to put in the Western woman's food and drink. The sehirra said the woman will curse us, and she was right. She has brought trouble here."

"She's not right—"

"Look how the she writhes. She's sick—"

"Because you poisoned her," Tair thundered, cutting Ashraf short. "You poisoned her food and drink and she writhes with physical pain, not with some mystical spirit. You gave her poisonous herbs to kill her and you are lucky that I do not give you some of the same."

"Ah! But see, you've just proven my point. Look what this woman has already done to us. Look at the evil she's brought on us. You're going to kill me and she what…will live here with you? How is that justice? How is keeping her and losing me right? Will she protect you as I have? Will she watch your back? No. She is bad and I tell you now, I warn you, brother to brother, man to man, not to keep her. She is a danger to all."

Tair let his other men take Ashraf away then.

Ashraf was wrong, Tair thought, watching the bound Ashraf settle onto his horse. Tair wasn't going to kill Ashraf, and Tally wasn't going to bring destruction on them. But things were getting complicated. As well as interesting.

Tally was sick, very sick, that much she understood, everything coming at her in a blur of heat and haze. She saw as if underwater, the world blurry and shapes shimmering toward her and then away. Even the voices she heard were like voices beneath the water, blah blah blah, strange tones and all jumbled sound. She tried to focus, tried to make sense of the noise and blur but it was too hard, too much effort and closing her eyes she gave up, returning instead to the bliss of sleep.

Tair stood over her bed, watching his woman sleep. The fever had finally broken. She was no longer thrashing so violently—thank Allah—but it'd been a difficult several days, days where he wondered over and over if he should air evacuate her to the hospital in Atiq but the doctor he'd sent for assured him she'd eventually respond to the treatment, and she had.

But there had been a night where Tair had doubted the doctor, threatening the physician with bodily harm if anything happened to his woman.

His woman.

A muscle in Tair's cheek pulled, a grim acknowledgment of a truth he was still coming to grips with. Somehow through the sandstorms and quicksand, knives and asthma attacks, he'd come to see her as his.

His responsibility. His duty. His fate. Whatever that meant.

And now that she was out of danger he'd have to break the news to her. She wouldn't like what he had to tell her. Not the first bit—she'd been poisoned. Or the second part—the culprit had been discovered and punished. Or the third—and he'd come to a decision.

It was time. To bring her home, introduce her to his people, make her his. He wasn't sure if they'd accept her but he had to find out now, before it was too late.

Two days later, Tally stared at Tair uncomprehendingly after he broke the news. "We're going to your home? To meet your people," she repeated slowly. "But I thought this was your home, and these your people."

"This is just a military outpost."

"An outpost!"

"One of three strategic positions that protect our people and territory."

Tally struggled to sit up, her body still weak. Shaky. "You've kept me in a military outpost instead of your home because...?"

"I didn't know if I could trust you."

"And now you can?"

"Yes."

"Why? Because I survived being poisoned by the belladonna flower?"

Tair grimaced. "No. Because I've been through your photos. All five hundred of them. And you were right. They're all of children." He paused, looked chagrined. "They're good, too."

Tally put a hand to her head, touched her forehead as if checking the temperature. "I'm hallucinating. Dreaming. Right?"

"No. You're sitting up and your eyes are open. You're quite awake."

Tally slowly lay back down again, and closed her eyes. "You liked my photos."

"Yes."

"And that's why I'm going to your real home?"

"I know you're not a spy."

She pushed up on one elbow. "Then maybe instead of dragging me across the desert to another horrible place I don't want to go, why don't you let me return to town? I'd love to have my things back. I miss my clothes more than you know."

"You'll like my home."

"Tair."

"It's pleasant there."

"Tair."

"It's already decided. Conserve your strength for the trip."

Tally's eyes fluttered closed, even as it crossed her mind that she rather liked the fever and delirium better than this wretched return to reality. Tair had no intention of ever returning her to Baraka, did he? If he had his way she'd live in Ouaha forever, wouldn't she?

"I'll have to kill you," she said dully, filled with weary resignation. "It won't be easy, but it must be done."

The tent was silent and for a long moment Tally held her breath, waiting for his response. And then it came. He laughed softly. "Good luck."

Two more days passed before Tair announced that they would be leaving in the morning. "I know you aren't completely recovered—"

"I'm fine," she interrupted, cutting him short.

"—so you will travel with me, on my horse," he continued as though she'd never spoken. "It will be a long day, we'll leave early, but we shall reach Bur Juman before dusk."

"Bur Juman?"

"Home."

Tally blinked, confused. "I thought this was your home."

Tair's hard features shifted, his firm mouth easing into a faint mocking smile. "This was a test."

"A test?"

He shrugged nonchalantly. "Now you will see where I live."

Tair was right. It was a long day traveling, and sitting so close to Tair on his horse made her even more restless than her fevers and delirium. The constant motion of the horse shifted her back and forth against Tair until every nerve ending felt rubbed raw.

Just when Tally didn't think she could handle another moment of such intimate contact, something took shape on the horizon. It wasn't cloud or wind. Wasn't a sandstorm or anything sinister. It was a mountain.

"Is that where we're going?" Tally asked, turning to look at Tair.

"Just wait," he answered.

It was a long wait. Another hour or more of riding but the

mountain grew larger and little by little Tally could see that the mountain was actually a mammoth rock jutting from the earth.

Tair and his men rode toward the rock, and then around the base of the rock and where there was a narrow ravine, they nudged their horses forward.

"Where are we going?" Tally whispered, awed by the sheer size of the rock soaring above them.

"You'll see."

And then she did.

Tally leaned forward on the horse, craning her head to get a better look.

This, she thought awed, was more like it.

This was a secret world Westerners were rarely permitted to see, a fantasy world carved from desert and wind, storm and age.

Tally tried to hide her excitement as the mountain opened up before her eyes. Tair's home appeared to be carved from rock—right from the mountain itself.

There were rooms marked by windows, shutters and iron grillwork, and then there were terraces, balconies, patios and stairs everywhere. Wooden staircases, ladders, wide stone steps, curving stone staircases. It was a fantasy world that was also home. Incredible. Like Swiss Family Robinson but only better because it was real. And she was here.

She felt Tair's gaze rest on her, felt his hard, male amusement.

"You like it," he said.

She shrugged indifferently. "It's…interesting."

"You should learn to lie better. Especially if you're going to lie as often as you do."

Tally pressed the tip of her tongue to the back of her teeth, pressing hard enough to feel the seam between her teeth and the little ridges high near her gums. "Why hasn't anyone put a poisonous snake in your bed yet?" she asked sweetly.

"They've tried."

She snorted, part laughter, part exasperation. "Just how many times have people tried to kill you?"

He crossed his arms, half-closed his eyes, counting. "Ten. Fifteen. Something like that."

"Come on. I'm being serious."

"You're right. It's higher than that. Probably closer to twenty. But I try not to dwell on negative things."

Tally shot him a look of disbelief before seeing the smile in his eyes. It was amazing how he could do that. His face was rigid—marble-like—and yet his eyes were so fierce and alive. And lately those beautifully alive eyes had been smiling.

"I'm so not surprised," she teased as gates were opened and men appeared to take the horses.

Tair greeted those who'd come to welcome him and then turned back to Tally. "Are you tired? Do you need to sit?"

"I've been sitting for hours."

"Yes, well, you're a weak sickly woman—" he broke off with a grunt as Tally's elbow made contact with his ribs.

"I wasn't that sickly until I was poisoned."

"And the asthma?"

"You don't want another one of these, do you?" she asked, pointing to her elbow.

"Indeed not. It's a dangerous weapon. One you actually know how to use." He led her to a wide stone staircase. They took the steps slowly and Tair talked as they climbed.

"This is Bur Juman." His voice was toneless and yet she heard his pride, as well as possession. "It was my father's home, and his father's home before that. For one hundred years my family and our people have lived here."

"Bur Juman," he said, pausing at the top of the staircase "means Pearl on the Other Side."

Tally immediately got the significance of the name. Pearl on the other side. This beautiful retreat of sun drenched stone patios and terraces was a world away from the dangerous desert they'd left, a world dominated by barbarians much like Tair

And yet here, this was a world of beauty, of women, of jewelry and ornamentation. The women were all hennaed, draped in gold, gold bracelets, necklaces, earrings, gold everywhere. Even the air around the women smelled sweet, perfumed by some indefinable Arabic scent that she'd caught whiffs of in town but here the fragrance permeated the very air, rivaling even the cloying sweetness of lemon and orange blossoms.

Pearl on the other side. Yes, definitely and Tally felt almost overwhelmed by the sensual beauty of it, ensnared by mystery and that which was new, different, exotic.

It was even harder to fathom coming as she and Tair had from the Spartan conditions of the desert camp. The encampment had been eerily desolate, deprived of women, softness, comfort of any sort. There were the men, the animals—goats, horses, the one scrawny dog that followed Tair everywhere—but no families, no children, no cry of babies or murmur of elders talking.

"Your men," she said, comparing the encampment to this stunning city cut from the cliffs, "this is their real home, isn't it?"

Tair turned, looked at her. For a moment he didn't speak, then just when she thought he wouldn't answer, he said, "My men choose to live apart from their families part of each year to better protect them. It's a choice they make. I've never insisted or dictated. They do it because they know they must."

"You rotate the men?"

"Regularly. It is hard on them—on the wives and children, too—when they are gone. But this is life on the border.

"Thirsty?" he asked.

Tally nodded. "Very."

"We'll have tea in my orange garden," he said, gesturing up one gently curving staircase carved from the peach colored stone of the mountain. "There's a private room and bath off the garden. Your attending girl will be waiting for you there."

A private room? A bath? A garden? Tally felt like she'd died and gone to heaven. She nearly clapped her hands. "This is wonderful here. Really lovely. Now if I could only have my camera back with the film," she concluded wistfully.

"You can," Tair said. "I'll have both brought to you later tonight."

Tally spun to face him. "Are you serious? You're giving me my camera and all the pictures back?"

"Yes."

"I can take pictures again…pictures here?"

He nodded gravely. "Yes."

Tally nearly hugged him. "That's fantastic, absolutely fantastic. You don't know how happy you've made me. Thank you." She beamed, impulsively touched his arm. "Thank you."

"My pleasure."

She rocked back on her heels. "So you believe me now. You know I'm a photographer, and trustworthy."

"Tally—"

"I'd love to take pictures here. But if you don't want me to photograph the children, I understand. And even if you don't want me to photograph the children, I'll still send you copies of the photos I take when I'm home—"

"Tally."

His curt tone cut through her bubble of happiness. She broke off, looked at him, saw the shadows in his eyes and the fierce lines in his face. He looked like the old Tair, the one who was more monster than man. "What?"

"This is home now."

She stared at him not understanding. She tried to hang on to her smile but it wobbled, disappeared. "You said that about the camp, Tair."

He didn't answer.

Tally's mouth dried. She swallowed quickly. "You said you trusted me. You said you knew I was a photographer, and you liked my photos. You said they were good."

"They are."

"Then what do you mean this is home. Tell me what you mean by that."

"I mean, this is where you'll live now. This is your home now, here at Bur Juman, with me."

"No. You can't mean it. You can't." The words burst from Tally in an impassioned frenzy. "You might say you're a brutal, vengeful, violent man, but I don't see it. Your men adore you—"

"Please don't say my men and adore in the same sentence. It makes me extremely uncomfortable."

"The point is, you know your men care about you."

"You're confusing affection and respect. My men don't care about me. They fear me. Two significantly different things."

"And why would they fear you?"

"They know the facts."

Tair sighed inwardly as he saw Tally's expression harden. He was familiar with women's emotional tendencies, understood they valued connection and relationships over logic and accomplishment, but this one, this woman, defied logic altogether.

He'd kidnapped her from the medina. He'd dragged her across the desert. He was holding her against her will and fully intended to keep her here. What about those actions symbolized tenderness or kindness? Where was the empathy? The compassion?

"Do not think you can change me," he said tersely, irritated to even be having this conversation. He was not a conversational man. Tally should know that by now. She should know him by now. "Do not imagine you can somehow shape me into a better, kinder version of me. It will not happen."

"I've no desire to change you. The only thing I want is to get out of here. Go home."

"Which I'm not going to allow you to do."

"So, let me get this straight. You've no intention of becoming the least bit likable, and I've got to spend forever here, too?"

Tair nearly smiled. Finally she sounded properly horrified. Now this was conversation he liked. "Yes. Exactly. I will not change. I will never be likable. And you will never be returned to your people."

A small muscle jumped in her jaw, near her ear. Her expression subtly tensed. "You mean, I won't be returned until I agree to erase all the camera's memory."

Tair didn't reply immediately, too intent on studying her eyes, where the sunlight shone, reflecting glints of green and gray and brown. He loved the color of her eyes. They reminded him of the part of Europe he loved, the old forests and cool woodland glens, the river beds filled with polished pebbles against banks softened by violets and ferns. In her eyes he remembered swimming in sun dappled ponds and hiding inside hollowed tree stumps. He could smell the water, the sticky sap of trees, the softness of moss growing on the far side of trees.

He remembered his mother.

He remembered the boy.

He remembered innocence.

"If I give you all the disks now, let you erase them, destroy them, you will let me go." Tally's voice was firm but he heard the whisper of uncertainty. Suddenly she wasn't so sure. Suddenly she doubted him. Again.

As she should.

His gaze dropped from her eyes, over the satin cream and rose of her fine Western skin to her mouth. Her lips were full, wide, the color a dark-dusty pink which he'd thought initially was makeup, but knew now it was just the color of her skin.

Pink and cream, rose and ivory.

The color of his woman.

His woman. And he knew without a doubt what he'd suspected earlier. He'd never intended to return her, never planned to let her go back.

She was his woman. She was going to be his wife.

They'd been together long enough. It was a longer courtship than he'd had with his first wife.

It was time to make their relationship official. Time to announce that the foreigner would soon be his bride.

"Tair." Her tone was increasingly urgent. "I'll do it. Get my camera and memory cards now. Let's just do it. Destroy them and be done with it."

"No."

"No?"

He shrugged, increasingly comfortable. Easy now that he'd made his decision, or more correctly, recognized the decision he'd made when he first spotted Tally in the square. It was kismet, he understood now. Fate. He'd seen her and knew without understanding why, that he had to have her. She was supposed to be his. "You'll stay here with me."

"I won't, Tair, and you know me. I'll run."

He shrugged again, unruffled. "And I'll come find you."

Her head turned and she looked at him from the corner of her eye. "Don't do this," she said softly, the warning clear enough in her voice.

"It's already done. You're here. We're together. I shall announce our marriage—"

"Marriage?"

"You shall be my second wife."

"And your first?"

"Dead."

Her mouth opened, closed and she put fingertips to her forehead where everything seemed fuzzy. Heatstroke. That's what it was. She was suffering heatstroke. "I will never marry you."

"There's no real ceremony. Nothing you have to do—"

"That's not the point."

"—so I say the words, announce it to my people, and it is done. You are my wife."

"Your wife."

"It is not such a very big step. Everyone already knows you

are mine. We are merely making official what is widely assumed. That you are my woman."

Tally honestly thought she was going to faint.

If only she could faint. If only she could slide to the floor and not have to listen to another word. But maybe in her dead faint he'd wave his hand over her and do his hocus-pocus wedding ceremony and then she'd really truly be in trouble then.

No, she couldn't faint. She had to stay calm and find a way out of here. Marry Tair? Be a sheikh's bride? Never.

CHAPTER EIGHT

THEY didn't end up having tea, at least, not together. Tally was too upset and Tair wasn't in the mood to coddle her. It'd be so much more convenient if she knew who he was. If she understood his power. His name. His reputation.

His reputation.

Leaving his stables where he'd checked that all the horses had been properly seen to, Tair slowly ran his thumb across his jaw, rubbing slowly, thoughtfully over the squared chin.

Tally didn't know his reputation but she should. She should know the kind of man he was. She should know what he'd done, what he'd do, without the least bit of remorse.

He was proud of his nature, comfortable being the warrior. The aggressor.

Bandit. King. Thief. King.

His lips pressed as he inhaled, nostrils pinching.

He'd lived too long to be timid, suffered too much to be gentle, risked too much to be sympathetic. Perhaps there were other men in his tribe, future leaders who'd be more temperate—just—but that was not him.

He wasn't kind, or generous. Neither patient nor sensitive.

He stole. He demanded. He insisted. And that was the way it was. He was also a man who had vowed to protect Tally now she was his.

And his Tally would be wise to accept the truth, and facts, fast.

* * *

Exhausted from the trip, Tally had hoped she'd fall into bed and sleep one of those deep dreamless sleeps but no, sleep wouldn't come and she spent hours tossing and turning in her bedroom high in Tair's personal tower.

Rolling over onto her back, she punched her pillow behind her head and took a deep breath, trying to calm herself.

It wasn't that getting married or being a wife was so distasteful. It was the way Tair did everything. It was his high-handedness, his authority, his insensitivity. It was the fact that he *insisted* it be done.

First of all, marriage wasn't a solution. Tally had lived enough years to know that love and relationships were important, but marriage was more of a problem then a solution. Marriage meant compromise, loss, sacrifice, and maybe someday she'd be ready to settle down, scale back her aspirations, give up some dreams but she wasn't there yet. Wasn't ready. There was still so much she needed to see, so much she wanted to do. Tally knew she had it in her to be a good mother—someday.

Someday. As in five, ten years from now.

Impulsively Tally left her bed. She knew where Tair's room was. His room was just doors from hers, on the same floor. Slipping a silk robe over her nightgown she went there now.

Tally knocked softly. "Tair?"

He called for her to enter.

His lamp was on and he was stretched out on his bed, shirtless, reading the first of an enormous stack of newspapers. His room was considerably cooler than hers with the tall glass paned doors open to the night.

"Can't sleep," she said nervously, glancing at his thickly muscled chest, and the scars over his heart, before looking away. The scars troubled her. Made her afraid for him somehow. "Am I bothering you?"

"No," he said, folding the paper he was reading in half, watching her approach.

She moved round the side of the bed. There were no chairs near the bed, just two nightstands heaped with books and more books. She glanced at the spines of one stack of books. The titles were all different, most foreign and it was like viewing the entries in an international film festival—French, English, Arabic, Italian.

Tally picked up a book from his nightstand, studied the cover. *Theory of Economics: Supply and Demand in Agrarian Society.* "Nice, light reading," she noted, returning the book to top of the stack. "Are they all like this?"

"There's a comfortable mix of history, politics and economics."

She bit her lip, wondered how on earth to start. The beginning, yes, but what was the beginning?

"Something's on your mind," he said.

"Yes." She suddenly wasn't sure she could do this after all.

"So tell me what's on your mind." He set the paper aside. "Or let me guess. You're angry about the wedding plans. You don't want to marry me. And you've no intention of staying here and spending the rest of your life at Bur Juman. How's that?"

"Pretty good."

He patted the side of his bed. "Sit."

Tally sat on the foot of the bed, taking a seat as far from him as she could. "So you know why I can't do this."

His gaze met hers. "I know why you can't leave." His gaze never wavered. "Tally, you know too much about us."

"Too much?"

"You have seen where we live, and work. You have seen the most private aspects of our lives. I can not send you back now. I can not risk my people's safety."

"I'm no risk. Surely you can see for yourself. You are a leader. You must be able to read people. You must be able to see the truth. I am not a dangerous person. I'm a good person."

"But even good can turn to bad."

"Not me. If I'd gone bad, I would have been years ago. But

I've always done the right thing, the good thing. I love art, and nature, books and adventure, and more than anything peace."

Tair's cheek pulled, a grim hint of a smile. "Are you sure you're not a politician?"

Tally made a soft sound of protest. "I know this much—you wouldn't have saved me three times if I was a bad person. You risked your own life three times for me. That means something."

Tair didn't move, just his lashes lowered, and yet he seemed harder, tougher. "Maybe here you pose no threat, but if I send you back to Baraka…" His voice drifted off.

He seemed to think he'd conveyed something very important, something earth shattering but she didn't have a clue as to what it was. "How does it change in Baraka?"

"In the wrong hands, you would be dangerous."

He was just confusing her. "I don't understand what you mean about the wrong hands?"

"I have enemies, *laeela*. We have enemies and I work very hard to protect my people. The women, the elderly, the children."

"But I would never hurt them—"

"Of course you wouldn't. But the problem isn't your camera or the photos anymore. It's you. Your mind. Your memory. The pictures in your head. In the wrong hands, with enough pressure—coercion—you could reveal things that would cause us all great harm."

Tally turned away, went to the window where night cloaked Tair's walled mountain city. Earlier the sunset had painted the city red and pink before fading to violet but now it was dark and she could only see dim murky shapes.

Pressing her hand to her cheek, her palm felt so hot against her skin, her cheek cold, cold, cold like the rest of her. "I can not live here forever," she whispered. "I can not stay here. This would be death for me. This would be nothing short of prison."

She didn't hear him leave the bed but suddenly his hands

were on her shoulders. Firm, but not heavy, steady, but with-out pressure. "You do not know the meaning of death, then," he said nearly as quietly. "Bur Juman is not death. Even prison is not death. Death is death. Death is death and nothing else."

She felt her eyes burn, her throat ache as if swelling closed. "My life is spent traveling. I live in hotels. I never stay in the same place long, never spend more than a week in the same city. I just can't live another type of life anymore."

His hands fell away. "Maybe it is time you stayed in one place."

"No!" She faced him, turning swiftly, passionately, her in-sides hot, as if on fire. "I am not ready to stay put. I am not ready to give up my life, or my work."

"But you're not a child anymore. You're a woman. Thirty-one. It is time for you to have children. You must have babies before you are too old."

Tally nearly choked on her own tongue, words strangling inside her throat. "I have only just started my career. Everything is still so new. I refuse to end my life here!"

"Marrying me, having children is not ending your life. It's a beginning. A beginning at Bur Juman. A beginning with me."

And that, she thought, pulling away from him, was no be-ginning at all. "We barely like each other," she flashed, fac-ing him.

"It's not necessary."

"Not necessary? You're talking about marriage."

"Wives don't need to like their husbands. They just need to obey."

Tally spun on her heel, clapped her hands on top of her head and walked the length of the room. This was ridiculous, the most ridiculous conversation she'd had yet, and she'd had many ridiculous conversations with Sheikh Tair lately, but this, oh, this took the cake.

Good God. Marry Tair? Live forever in his desert? Not just have his children but *obey* him?

Tally almost laughed, hysteria building. "You do not know me well, do you?" she spluttered, hands still on top of her head, fingers locked down against her scalp. It was that or let her panic spill out. "I am not the stay home and have babies kind of woman. I climb and run and swim and—" she broke off, dragged in air "—*not* have babies. And *not* obey." She looked at him, trying to make him understand. "I don't obey."

His eyebrows lifted and his lips pursed. "Not very well, no."

"Not at all." She exhaled again. "So save us both endless frustration and disappointment. Get me to the next big city and put me on an international flight home. I won't even stop to buy postcards. I'll just go. I'm out of here. I won't even look back—"

"Bur Juman is a beautiful place to live."

"For Berbers or Bedouin, or whatever you are."

His lips pinched. "I have much to teach you."

"But I don't want to be taught. I've had enough lessons from you, and my family, and everyone else who thinks they know what's best for me. But no one knows what's best for me but me."

Tair sighed deeply. Silence stretched between them, heavy and heavier. Tally's fingers knotted into her palms and silently she prayed, prayed he'd come to his senses and do what was right, do what he needed to do.

"Yes," he said at last, "it is going to be a very hard marriage. And I'm afraid, a very long life."

He joined her for breakfast on the stone terrace that adjoined her room. "Sabah-ul-kher," he greeted, taking the low stool across from her and reaching for one of the tangerines and then one of the pomegranate sections. "How did you sleep?"

Tally gave him a baleful look. "Not particularly well, thank you."

"You might want to take a rest later today. You're still on the weak side—"

"Tair—"

"My delicate little flower." His dark eyes flashed with amusement.

Tally marveled at the pleasure he derived from her misery. "Why are you so happy? You're like a different man now you're back in your palace."

He peeled the tangerine, bit into one bright orange wedge and offered her a piece. Tally shook her head. Tair ate another, wiped his hands and asked, "Do you have a preference for your robe for the wedding?"

He was serious about this. He was moving ahead with plans for a wedding. "You can't make me marry you. You can't."

"I can, actually. I'm a sheikh. You're part of my harem—"

"I'm not."

"Harem doesn't mean a dancing girl, Tally Woman. It means part of one's household."

"So I'm like cutlery or dish towels, is that it?"

"More or less." His mouth curved, eyes glinting, baiting her. "You know, marrying me is in your best interest."

"No, Tair, it's not. It's in your best interest."

And then he did what he always did. That horrible, arrogant, infuriating shrug. "So it is."

Tair looked up as the serving girl brought him hot coffee. He thanked her and the girl flushed, pink with pleasure. Tally groaned inwardly. Everybody loved Tair but her.

He turned his attention back to her. "You haven't given me your preferences for your robe for the ceremony yet. Surely you'd like to select that yourself."

"I didn't realize your attractive robes came in a number of different colors and designs," Tally answered with mock sweetness. "So far I've only seen basic black and basic white."

"There is a lovely shade of blue."

"*Navy.*"

He tipped his head. "See."

"So you're asking if I'd like to be married in black, white, or blue?"

A muscle popped in his jaw. "Yes."

"Hmph." She couldn't believe how much he irritated her, infuriated her, couldn't believe he really thought they could marry, spend time together, much less time in bed!

At thirty-one she was no simpering virgin, but she'd never managed to look at sex as recreational activity, either. Sport was sport, and sex was well, private. Intimate. Sex was making love. And how was she supposed to make love with a man she didn't even respect?

Tally lifted her chin, forced a tight smile. "Surprise me. It will make the wedding day such a delight."

Tair suddenly reached for her wrist, fingers encircling her slender bones and he pulled her up, to her feet, and then around the table toward him. "You're such a feisty bride to be."

She tugged hard, resisting. "Because you're so not the groom I ever wanted."

He dropped her into his lap. "Why?"

His thumb was slowly, lazily drawing circles on the inside of her wrist. It was annoying. Distracting. Disturbing. Little forks of sensation raced through her arm, licks of fire and ice that tingled from her arm to her middle, curling hotly in her belly. Damn him. He couldn't arouse her. She wouldn't let him arouse her. She had no wish to be aroused by Tair of the Desert. He was horrible. Uncivilized. Barbaric.

"You know why," she said gruffly.

"Because I'm a sheikh?"

She growled a protest. *"No.* It's not cultural, or religious—it's you. You. You stole me, kidnapped me, imprisoned me. Why would I want to marry you?" Then she shuddered, shivering not from distaste but the unnerving things his touch was doing to her. He shouldn't be able to make her feel anything. She didn't like him. Didn't admire him. Didn't want him.

But oh, and she shivered again, a ripple of helpless response as his thumb stroked over and over that little sensitive pulse point on her wrist. Problem was, that little sensitive spot seemed to be growing. Her whole arm had come alive, her skin flushed, her body tensing in protest.

Delicious protest.

Tally's brows pulled, flattened. Damn him. How could she ever respect him if he didn't even let her respect herself? A man that broke down her defenses with touch—with pleasure—well, that was just wrong.

They should talk. Converse. Even play a game of chess. But touch? So brutally unfair.

"And if I hadn't kidnapped you? You'd like me then?"

She couldn't meet his eye. "Maybe."

"Woman, I think not," he scoffed.

Woman. She clenched her teeth. Why did he still call her that? He knew she hated it. He knew she hated his chauvinistic attitude, but did he change? No. Would he ever change? *No.*

"You're right," she fumed. "Even if I'd met you at a cocktail party at the Barakan Embassy I wouldn't like you. It's not political. It's personal, completely personal. You're everything I don't like in a man. Hard, mean-spirited, bullying."

She paused for breath before continuing. "A man should never try to dominate a woman and yet that's all you do. Dominate and push me around."

He leaned toward her, closing the distance so that she felt the warmth of his skin, the tension crackling between them. "I've saved you, too."

His mouth was so close, his lips just there above hers and she felt a sharp lance of pain, and it surprised her, the cut and twist in her chest and belly. Wrenched, that's how she felt. Wrenched.

"You were the one that put me in danger," she protested, voice hoarse. "It's only fair you saved me."

"I didn't put you in danger." He head dipped, his lips just missing hers to brush her cheek and then lightly touch the corner of her mouth. "You put yourself in danger by behaving in an emotional, impulsive, irrational manner."

She wanted to jerk away, wanted to pull back and escape but the feel of his mouth against her skin was so seductive it confused her, held her, made her want more.

How could she still hate him and yet feel so good when he touched her? How could her mind reject him and yet her body came up with a totally different assessment?

"You are bad," she whispered, voice thick, deep, tinged with a longing she couldn't reconcile herself to.

"You must like bad." He touched her face, fingers lightly stroking one cheek as his lips brushed the other.

"No."

"Mmmm."

She squeezed her eyes shut as silver streaks of sensation raced up and down her spine. "I'm good," she insisted.

She felt rather than heard him laugh softly, felt the rise and fall of his chest, the muffled humor. "So you keep saying."

She was just about to protest when his hands moved, and he cupped her jaw between his palms, holding her face up to him.

The air caught in Tally's throat and she stared up at him wide-eyed. This was as fantastic as it was awful and like a deer caught in headlights, she waited, waited, spellbound for disaster to hit.

And it did.

His head dropped, his lips covered hers and in that instant his mouth touched hers, she exhaled, resistance disappearing as she gave in to his warmth and scent and skin.

His kiss was again right, absolutely right, and maybe she couldn't marry him, and maybe she wouldn't live with him, but God, he knew how to kiss her. His kiss was amazing. She'd hoped it was just the first kiss that she responded to, hoped that having kissed him once, she would have become immune to him. But no, no immunity here. If anything it was even better.

Tally felt his arm slide around her waist and pull her against him and it was so right. Exciting and yet comforting.

It made her think, imagine, that somehow in his arms she was home. That somehow right now, like this, she'd found the only place she needed to be.

And like that, cold reality intruded, and Tally pulled abruptly away.

She stared at him accusingly, seeing him through hazy eyes. *"No."*

"No what?"

"No to everything." And yet inexplicably tears burned the back of her eyes. "No, you can't have me. No, I won't stay. No, I won't marry you. No."

He looked at her a long level moment than shrugged. "So it's a blue robe you want for the ceremony."

"Tair."

But he wasn't listening. He was lifting her off his lap and now he was standing. "I shall see what we can do."

"Tair!"

But he was walking, heading out the door. He didn't stop, turn, didn't respond. No, he just kept walking, leaving her alone with the memory of a kiss that burned and burned and burned some more. And it wasn't just her lips burning. It was her heart.

CHAPTER NINE

THE women want you to join them for coffee this morning.
Tair's voice echoed in her head as she made her way from her
suite of rooms to the rooftop on the far tower of the walled
city, that tower officially designated as the women's space.

Tally hesitantly entered through the high arched doorway,
the stone columns supporting the fancifully carved arch. She
heard a chorus of voices down a corridor and followed the
sound of the voices into a large chamber lined with low
benches and vibrant silk pillows and cushions.

Everyone stopped talking and turned to look at Tally when
she appeared. Tally hadn't been sure if she'd truly be welcome
but as she shyly entered the room the circle of women beamed
at Tally. *"Ahlen-wa-sehlan,"* one after another cried.
Welcome, welcome!

They bustled about, finding space for Tally among them
on the cushions on the floor. Flustered at the attention, Tally
sank onto one of the cushions and made a show of arranging
her robes, and pulling back the veil on her head so that her
long hair spilled down one shoulder.

Beautiful, one woman said, while another reached forward
to touch Tally's hair.

"Salaam," Tally greeted, nodding at one and all, trying to
ignore the flurry of nerves. There was no reason to be so fearful, she told herself. They wouldn't bite.

But they won't approve, either, she thought darkly, knowing that for a man like Sheikh el-Tayer, a man with such great power, a suitable marriage was one with a woman from his own people, a woman from his tribe.

The women were all still beaming at her, waiting, and Tally's smile wobbled a little. What if she never did leave? What if she couldn't escape?

Her forehead furrowed as she scanned the eager, open, curious faces of the women gathered. Her gaze lighted on one of the youngest women, visibly pregnant.

What if this place truly became home? Nodding, smiling, she accepted a small cup of Turkish coffee. Could she ever be happy here? Could these women become friends?

She didn't know. Tally bit the inside of her lip, fought the wave of confusion, realizing the only thing she was sure of was that these ladies deserved some place nicer than a rooftop and cemetery for socializing.

She kept coming back to anger. She couldn't get away from it. No matter what she did, no matter how she tried to occupy herself, the anger snuck in and colored everything.

Maybe Tair could be good company. Maybe they even had moments that were surreal—gorgeous, sensual, seductive—but in the end, they were just moments and reality barged in, reminding Tally about truth. Honor. Justice. Never mind respect.

The truth was men couldn't kidnap women. The truth was a man couldn't hold another human being hostage. The truth was she couldn't respect a man who refused to let her make decisions for herself…indeed, who forced his decisions on her.

This is why she couldn't like Tair, and wouldn't like Tair, and wouldn't calm down and wouldn't play nice, and wouldn't be the good girl and do as she was told.

She couldn't.

There had to be a line that one didn't cross. There had to be morals. Principles. Values. Tair was about neither.

Tair was about Tair.

She harrumphed beneath her breath, temper hot, spiking. It seemed to always be up lately, always heated about something.

Tair's effect on her world.

Tair should be kidnapped, she silently groused, scooting lower in bed, tipping her head back against the bright silk cushions, staring up at the dark carved bed canopy that had been lined with silk the color of orange marmalade.

The orange silk made her hungry and marmalade made her think of toast and toast made her think of tea and toast and tea made her wish she were back in her own apartment in Pioneer Square with her own kitchen and her own groceries. She hated relying on others, depending on others, hated not being able to do what she wanted when she wanted it.

Like now. She wanted food, a snack, wanted to wander out and about and not be sent to her room simply because it was late, and dark, and all good women went to their rooms now.

Tally reached for a crimson cushion, the corners heavily embroidered with gold and crimson beads and nearly tossed it across the room, but at the last second, didn't throw it. Clung to it.

Why couldn't she go get a snack? She knew the general vicinity of the kitchen. Why couldn't she get something because she was hungry?

Pushing the pillow aside, she slid off the bed, dragged a dark outer robe over her delicate teal gown and left her room in search of food and drink.

She didn't get far before a robed man noticed her. He didn't stop her though. Nor speak to her. He watched her, then stepped back and she continued on, walking down one hall and stairs to another floor where she encountered another man—Tair's guards?—and then another. Each time the men let her continue, none of them disturbing her, none of them saying a word, or giving her a look of reproof. Tally soon found out why.

Tair had been alerted—probably by the very first man she'd passed in the upper hallway—and was waiting for her downstairs.

"Running away?" he asked mildly.

"Hungry." She shot him a swift glance. "Is that allowed, my lord?"

"Oh, if only that were the case." He held out a hand, gestured for her to follow him. "But let me see if we can get someone to prepare something for you. Should only take a moment to wake one of the cooks."

"I don't want to wake the cooks—"

"Yet you're hungry."

"I know, but I can help myself. I like doing things myself."

"I'm afraid our kitchens aren't like yours in America. You'd find it difficult to get anything prepared."

"How about simple tea and toast?"

"I'll have the cook—"

"Forget it," Tally sighed, turning away and pushing a hand through her hair, lifting it off the back of her neck. She was hot. Hungry. Grouchy. Tonight the heat hadn't abated and she didn't want Tair's company and what she really wanted— was something comforting. Something that would calm her, relax her, make her feel like herself again.

"I'll just go back to my room," she said unenthusiastically, turning to retrace her steps and head back to her room on the third floor of the tower that wrapped around the mountain and gave expansive views of the desert valley beyond.

Tair fell into step beside her. "What's wrong?"

She grimaced. "What do you think is wrong? I'm hot, and hungry—I'm not used to eating goat and goat and goat—and I've no books, and nothing to write with, and no camera to play with." They were climbing the first staircase, their slippered feet silent on the worn stone steps. She lifted her hair off her neck again, exhaled a little, blowing the wisp of hair off her brow. "I'm bored. And trapped. And really really hot."

Tair's eyebrows lifted. "And you're hot."

"Yes."

"Hungry and hot."

"Yes."

"And tired?"

"No. Not tired. Just bored."

"Restless."

"Exactly." She paused on the second landing, her hand on the banister. "Tonight I just feel like a…" She glanced around, at the thick walls, and the iron bars on the lower windows. She shook her head. "A caged cat. And I hate feeling this way. I've spent too much time out—exploring—to feel comfortable all cooped up."

His lips twisted and for the first time in days his expression was almost sympathetic; something had changed in him. "You sound like one of my men who has been here at Bur Juman too long." His jaw shifted ruefully. "I have certain men who can only be here so long before they go stir-crazy."

"Stir-crazy," she echoed before shaking her head. "You know all the oddest expressions."

"My English education."

Tally lifted her head to search his face, trying to see past the wall he kept up, the wall that hid his thoughts and emotions from everyone around him. "You never talk about your education in England."

"I know." He gestured toward the next set of stairs. "Shall we?"

Resigned, Tally set up the next flight, torches flickering soft gold and orange light. She glanced at Tair once, and then again, wanting to push him for more information. She was fascinated by this side of him, the Western mother, the Western education, but he said so little *she* didn't really know what he knew. How he felt. And that brought her back to the wall he maintained, the wall that kept him so mysterious as well as aloof.

Tally hated the wall. Hated it so much she vowed to break

it down. She'd know him. She would. Even if it was the last thing she did.

On the third floor Tally turned toward her room when Tair's hand touched the small of her back. "Not yet," he said, his deep voice, so rough in the way he spoke his English, even deeper, rougher in the hollowed tunnels of the castle Tair called home. "I've something spectacular to show you."

Curiosity piqued, Tally followed.

Tair led her to the door of his room and when she balked at the entrance, he smiled mockingly down at her. "And just what do you think I'm going to show you? A part of my anatomy?"

Heat surged to her cheeks and she rolled her eyes. "No."

"It is spectacular," he added, his dark eyes glinting wickedly, "but it's not why I've brought you here. You won't get that lesson until our wedding day."

"Which will be never," she muttered beneath her breath.

"Not so," he corrected, "but for tonight, let's focus on this—" He pushed open his door, took her hand and led her through his room to the set of glass doors across the way.

Tally expected to go through the doors to a balcony much like hers, a balcony with a view of the desert and the endless vista of moonlit sand, but his room had French doors on both sides of the room and while one set of doors opened on the desert, there was another set that opened to a private patio— a huge patio, a virtual walled garden that shimmered in the moonlight. Shimmered.

It was a pool. A pool carved from the stone, a pool that must have been like something in Eden. So natural, so real, so…cool.

Tally felt immediate relief and she looked up at Tair who was watching her, smiling his faint knowing smile and then she looked back to the water. "You have your own pool."

"I am the sheikh."

Tally stood just inside the doorway staring at the glistening water. My God, this was like the VIP rooms at the elite hotels and clubs. This was the life she'd never known, a life she didn't think existed, a life carved from rock and on the surface arid, so dry, but in truth nothing like that. Tair's world was more seductive, more erotic than anything she'd found in Seattle or the Pacific Northwest. Tair's world was…indulgent.

And Tally, deprived of indulgences, found it horribly, shamefully attractive.

You won't be bought, Tally, she sternly reminded herself. You have better morals. Remember your scruples. Remember that high road, that's the one you decided to take.

But really, the high road was less interesting than what lay before her. The high road was hot and difficult, rough and lonely and God—what she wouldn't give to plunge into the pool and just float there, cool, calm, comfortable.

"Can I swim?" she asked, laying an impulsive hand on Tair's arm. "I don't have a suit but it's dark out and you won't see—" She broke off, remembered herself. Remembered him. "Unless you have a suit for me?"

"Not readily, no."

"So your lady friends don't keep suits here?" she asked, knowing she was being arch and unable to help it. She was curious after all.

"No." He closed the French doors, so that they were alone in his walled garden with the pool reflecting the very nearly full moon.

"They swim naked?" she persisted.

Tair moved toward her, took the outer robe in his hand and drew it off, over her head and dropped the dark fabric in a puddle at her feet. His gaze lowered, lingered, taking in the fullness of her curves beneath the thin silk of her aqua gown. "They swim naked."

Naked.

Tally sucked in air, heat flooding her limbs yet again.

The man had a way with words.

Trying to hide her flurry of nerves, Tally moved away from

him, walking to the edge of the pool. She crouched at the side, reached in, touched the water. Not hot like a spa, nor cold. Just perfect.

Staring toward the bottom she tried to make out the depth of the pool and she couldn't see the bottom, not easily. It wasn't a shallow pool. And it wasn't small. It was a pool one could swim in, exercise in.

Tally stood, dipped a toe into the water, the hem of her gown trailing in the water, too.

"You're getting your robe wet," he said, watching her from the shadows.

She smiled. "I don't have a suit."

"And so what are you going to do?"

Her smile stretched and she felt suddenly, surprisingly carefree. My God. She was here, she was okay, she was—and just like that, she dove into the pool, a shallow dive, not deep, just in case the pool was more shallow than she thought, but the water was perfect, so cool, so refreshing and Tally surfaced and turned over on her back and smiled up at the sky. She hadn't felt so free ever before.

"Look at all the stars." It was such a beautiful night. Stars and stars—galaxies of them.

Tair joined her at the pool, sat down on one of the low chairs at the pool's edge. "Better?"

"Yes." She turned over onto her stomach and kicked her feet to stay afloat. "This is bliss."

"Bliss?" His black eyebrows arched. "You're easily pleased."

"No. But this is amazing, you have to admit." She turned in a circle, gazed around the courtyard formed by mountain and castle, and the sole palm tree that arched above the pool in its small allotment of dirt. "You have a pool in the middle of a mountain."

"A man's got to do what a man's got to do."

Tally laughed. Not a fake laugh, not one of her tense

laughs, but a big belly laugh and the sound poured out, filling the moonlit, star filled night.

"I've never seen you so happy," Tair said after a moment, watching Tally slowly swim one length of the pool and then another.

"I feel free," she answered, turning easily onto her back to float, head back, eyes riveted on the indigo sky above, the heavens blue-black in places and fluorescent in others. So much sky. So many stars. So much life still ahead of her.

Her hands fluttered at her sides, small strokes to keep her floating.

As a kid in North Bend she used to sit in her backyard and stare up at the sky and make wishes and dream, and vow to get the life she'd never had, the life she'd always wanted, all the adventure, all the drama, all the great moments denied because she wasn't pretty and wasn't clever and her family was poor.

"When I was little I wanted to be a princess," she said, water lapping at her ears, making her voice sound hollow and far away. "I used to count the stars and make promises to myself. Someday I'd be beautiful. And someday I'd be famous. And someday I'd be rich." She sat up, her arms and legs circling, keeping her upright in the water. "I really thought if I could just be a princess—marry Prince Albert of Monaco or even one of Princess Diana's sons—I'd be happy."

Tair's dark gaze followed her in the night. "And you still think becoming a princess would help?"

She laughed softly. "No. I don't want to be a princess, but I still want a lot. I still want virtually everything."

Tair sat in a chair at the side of the pool and watched Tally float, her skin pale, pearl-like in the light of the moon.

She'd bewitched him. She with her hellcat ways, temper and tears. So full of fire, her spirit never seemed to break and the fact that she hadn't bowed to him—that, too—he welcomed, wanting a woman not a doormat. No matter how much he teased her.

He needed a woman like Tally, a woman to stand up to him, be honest with him, give her opinions. He'd been feared by so many, and women either adored him or ran in abject terror. He craved neither pedestal or absolute authority. A relationship was what he wanted, needed, a relationship with a woman like Tally.

Tally reminded him of a past he no longer knew, a past where he'd been fun, carefree, easy. When he was sent to England at six for school, it'd never crossed his mind that he'd return years later sheikh and leader. He'd never wanted to lead. It hadn't been his dream, or his vision. He'd loved sports. He'd loved studies. He'd loved fun.

Fun. The corner of his mouth lifted, his gaze resting on shimmering Tally. She made him want to join her, made him want to shed his robe and responsibility and just let go. Let go of power and duty long enough to live. Long enough to feel. Long enough to let go of the pain of the past and the man he had become.

But no. That couldn't be. Horrific things happened in life and Tair had to be prepared for every possibility, had to be aware, alert, vigilant.

Tair's first lesson in reality was his father's death. Summoned from the university in Cambridge, Tair came home to a changed world. A world where the West was bad, evil. A world where his father had been killed by a superpower sharpshooter. The jittery soldier had assumed Tair's father, Sheikh Hassem el-Tayer, was dangerous, a threat, and pulled a trigger too quickly. The foreign governments and their military offered perfunctory apologies but apologies don't bring men back from the dead.

As if the death of Tair's father wasn't hard enough, there were the border wars and the endless bloodshed, senseless bloodshed in Tair's estimation. Why should Arab be pitted against Arab? Why Berber against Bedouin? Tair had fought to remain impartial—fair—until the war came home while he was in Baraka on business.

The war shouldn't have come home. Ara should have listened to him. Ara should have obeyed. But no, his Ara had been proud, fierce, beautiful and so sure she could handle anything life threw at her.

Pain flickered through him, orange spots before his eyes and he curled the fingers of his right hand into a fist. All these years and he still remembered, all these years he felt the same shock and despair.

If Ara hadn't opened the gates for the others...if Ara had just done what he'd always told her to do. If she'd listened, if she'd been less brave...

Tair's hand opened and clenched again, and as he clenched his fist, the muscles corded all the way up his arm, tightening, squeezing.

He missed them. He'd missed his wife and son more than he could admit, more than he could bear.

Zaki in his arms, Zaki dying, Zaki's blood running, spilling, no way to save the child he'd loved from the moment of conception in his mother's womb.

Tair closed his eyes. *My son, I have never forgotten you. My son, I will never forget.*

"Tair."

The soft voice, warm, tender, whispered to him and for a moment he could have sworn it was Ara. Ara speaking.

"Tair. What are you thinking?"

But of course it wasn't Ara. Ara was dead.

He opened his eyes, and even though he knew Ara was gone, he half expected to see her standing there, Ara his brave heart, his courageous foolish dead wife.

"Tair." Tally had climbed from the pool and she was naked wet, shivering. "You're so far away. What are you thinking?"

Tair looked at her, slender, bare, beautiful woman and he

held out a hand to her and she came to him as if it were the most natural thing in the world. And maybe it was.

Tally felt Tair fold her to him and seconds ago she'd been cold, and yet in his arms she felt warm, nearly as warm as he was. Instinctively she lifted her face, wanting his kiss, needing his kiss, sensing that just maybe he needed her kiss, too. Men were so complicated and simple—male, hard, arrogant, but then tender on the inside with their profound need for a woman's touch. For a woman's love.

Hot tears burned the back of her eyes and a lump filled her throat as she felt Tair draw her closer, fitting her naked body to his. She ought to feel self-conscious, ought to feel strange with him but there was nothing strange in being held in his arms, or being close against his heart. He with his wounds across his chest had been wounded in other ways, and she didn't know what those wounds were but they mattered to her.

He mattered to her.

Maybe more than her own freedom.

CHAPTER TEN

WITH her still pressed to him, Tair began walking backward, leading her away from the pool and into his room.

As he walked, he kissed the side of her neck, just beneath her earlobe, and then worked his way down all the way to her collarbone. Hot forks of sensation raced through her and she couldn't suppress the shivers of pleasure.

She knew where he was going, seeing his great bed with the silk coverlet from the corner of her eye. "Is this wise?" she whispered, forced to cling to him, her legs weak as he kissed the rise of her collarbone and then the small hollow at her throat.

"Yes," he murmured against her skin, "very wise. I'm losing my patience with waiting to make you mine."

His deep rough voice hummed and vibrated through her. Her head spun, dizzy from her shallow breathing and yet she couldn't slow her pulse, her heart beating too hard and fast. Tally felt wild with desire and excitement. How was it possible to feel so much? She was exquisitely aware of his hands, his mouth, his warmth and frantically sucked in air as he cupped her breasts, letting the weight of them fill his hands.

There was something so seductive and yet so gratifying in his touch. She recognized him at a level that couldn't be explained. But she knew him in some deep primal part of her, knew him as a man, and her man. And yes, she thought, arms wrapping around his neck, her skin alive, body rippling, she was his. His.

Tally pressed closer, impatiently unbuttoning his shirt to kiss the warm spice-scented skin that stretched across his chest, the warm fragrant skin just above the scars. She'd never been bold with men but Tair made her brave, Tair made her want to seize all the life she could and make it hers, including sex, if not love. And opening his shirt wider, she touched her lips to the scars marring his chest thinking this is where she wanted him to want her, carry her, here in his heart.

His horrible awful barbarian heart.

The heart she wanted more than anything.

He lifted his head to look down into her eyes. "You know you're mine. You know there's no leaving me. This is where you belong. You know this now."

His words rushed over her, through her, even as his voice hummed in her veins and skin. It was hard to think clearly, hard to think of anything at all but getting closer, eliminating the last bit of distance between them. She needed him, not just his mouth and mind, but his body, his powerful fearsome body with the corded tendons and rippling strength, the biceps and quadriceps, the roping of muscle beneath bronzed warrior skin.

"I claim you," he added, hands sliding down her back to clasp her buttocks, and hold her firm against his hips where his erection pressed thick and hard against her belly. "Don't think you can change this. Don't think you can run away now."

Her eyes closed as she felt his fingers grasp her bottom, the pressure of his hands on her tender skin. His hands were warm and they made her feel hot and madly empty. She wanted those hands on her everywhere, wanted those hands to take her, and even take her apart like a tower of children's building blocks and then put her back together again.

"You won't run away," he insisted, hands moving between her legs, touching her lightly, intimately.

She shuddered and nodded blindly. Nothing he said registered. Everything he said registered. He'd become all, primal and sexual and male. Her male. The one that made her shiver and shudder. The one that had set loose this firestorm of need. As he touched and stroked she arched, breasts crushed against his chest, hips swaying to a silent tattoo of hunger, a hunger she desperately needed him to appease. "Yes," she choked.

"Yes, what?" he demanded, bending her back over his arm to look at her, see her, the woman he would soon possess as only he could possess.

"I won't run away," she said, voice husky, feeling her breasts tighten at the rush of cool air, her nipples ruche, peak.

Tair couldn't fail to notice her response and his gaze dropped appreciatively, resting on the ripe swell of her rose-tipped breasts.

Tally had been eyed by men before, but it had never felt like this. This was ownership, a claiming that burned all the way to her soul.

His dark head dipped, thick black hair hiding his face as his mouth touched her breast and then her nipple, his lips parting to take the aching peak into his mouth, against his tongue and teeth. He tugged at the sensitive flesh and she moaned deep in her throat as he licked, bit, teased until she was trembling, her nerves taut, tauter. She was melting and craving and needing and shuddering Tally pressed herself closer.

She needed him. Needed to appease that hollow feel inside of her, her body hot, and yet increasingly empty.

They'd reached his bed and Tair pushed her down on his bed cool and smooth with luxurious silk coverings. Tally reached for the front of his shirt and pulled him down to her, on her.

"But I want to look," he said, drawing back.

"Yes, but I want to feel," she answered, cupping the back of his head and bringing his face to hers. Her eyes closed as his lips covered hers, the sensation again electric. His kiss felt unlike any kiss she'd ever known before.

Tair stroked the length of her and when she couldn't stand the coiled tension inside her any longer she tugged at his robe, and then his trousers wanting him naked.

Lashes lowered, Tally watched Tair strip, her breath catching in her throat as all the clothes came off and he was even harder, prouder, more gorgeous than she'd expected. He was all muscle and sun-tarnished skin, smooth, cut, fiercely made. She'd seen men with gym-toned bodies but Tair's was shaped by life and battle, desert, wind and sun and she knew then she loved him, knew she loved him in a way she hadn't thought possible.

He was the man she'd been searching for. He was the love she'd looked for all these years.

Stinging tears filled her eyes and she blinked them away before Tair could see.

"Come to me," she whispered, reaching up to take his hand.

Tair's eyes were dark, nearly black and the expression in them scorched her.

He was all fire and danger and she was running straight into the flames. She was tugging him down to her and as he settled over her, he parted her thighs with his own. She muffled a groan as he explored the indentation of her waist and then the flare of her hips and over her hip bones to her flat belly. Every place he touched grew hot, while her insides felt wicked, liquid, hungry for him. Ready.

But Tair wouldn't be rushed. He seemed to delight in her body, in the curves and shapes, the softness of her skin, the pale globes of her breasts, the shadow between her thighs. And as he explored, he paid attention to each of her soft gasps, remembering what she liked, how she responded so that he could play her as if she were an instrument and his alone to enjoy.

Tally felt mad with all the sensation. No one had ever touched her like this, making her want at so many levels, making her body feel both familiar and strange. She'd never thought she was passionate, or physical but as Tair cupped her full breasts, his thumbs grazing her nipples, all self-consciousness fell away. She'd do anything for him, anything with him. Somehow he'd found a way into her heart and now her body wanted him, to be joined with him, now and forever.

He entered her with a smooth, hard thrust, confidence in the way he took her, confidence in the way he moved in her and Tally wrapped her arms around him, her heart and mind and body wanting him like she'd never wanted anyone.

An expert lover, Tair took her to the highest pinnacle of pleasure, driving her to the point of no return and beyond until she shattered in a thousand iridescent pieces, falling apart in his arms, held safely by him in great arms against a hard, muscular chest.

With her body still trembling she laced her fingers through his and held on. If only this moment could last forever. If only she could feel this way always…

Heart thudding, Tally pressed her cheek to his chest just above his heart. She could feel the scar tissue from his wounds against her cheek even as his powerful heart beat a steady rhythm against her ear.

All she wanted now was to hold him, touch him, remember. Remember not just him, but the way it felt to be held like this. Closing her eyes, she tried to memorize every muscle, imprinting his warmth and strength and scent in the deepest part of her.

"You are a very complicated woman." Tair's voice rumbled from him and idly he lifted a heavy strand of hair back and drew it from her face. "And yet when I hold you like this, you are so simple. You make perfect sense."

"I could say the same for you."

He suddenly lifted her, moving her higher on his body, up into his arms so that he could better see her face. "You're beautiful. I'll always marvel at the way you were put together." He grasped her jaw, lifted her face, studying it in the candlelight. "This jaw, the nose, the cheekbones, such wide clear eyes. Such clear intelligent eyes. You must know your beauty. The effect you have on men."

"I've no effect on men."

"No effect? You've turned my life upside down, Woman. I've chased after you across the desert far too many times to count—"

"Two actually."

"How you love to have the last word."

"No more than you do."

"There you go again."

Smiling, she clasped his face and kissed him deeply, giving him her heart not with words but actions. He had to know how she felt about him. He had to know that she couldn't imagine not being here, not being his. "Maybe just a little of what you say is true," she whispered against his mouth.

He laughed softly, the sound of deep rumble in his chest. "So you've finally come to your senses."

Tally loved the feel of his chest against her own and the way her legs tangled with his. If this is life this is all she wanted. To be loved and held. Kept. Savored. Treasured. "I think you've taken my senses, that's what I think."

Laughter rumbled through him again and the sound was alien and yet right. Tair should laugh more, she thought. Tair deserved more happiness and turning her head, she found his hand and kissed his palm. "Make love to me again." Her gaze lifted, her eyes met his and her lips curved slightly. "Please."

Tally spent the night in his bed, sleeping close to his side, his arm around her waist holding her firmly against him. He was warm and hard and she found it difficult to sleep with his big body so close to hers but it was a wonderful strangeness, the kind of strangeness that brought comfort. Peace.

Peace.

And holding that warmth and peace in her heart she finally closed her eyes and fell asleep. Life was good and life could only get better.

* * *

Tally's feeling of goodwill did not last long. When she woke she discovered that Tair was gone, and not just out of the bed gone, but gone gone. He and a number of his men had left for El Saroush and wouldn't be back for days. Maybe a week. *A week!*

Back in her room, Tally paced the room, her bare feet silent on the thick wool and cashmere rug. Why hadn't he told her he was leaving? He'd had plenty of time last night to update her with his schedule. Or did he think she wouldn't be interested? That she had so many friends and interests here at Bur Juman that she wouldn't notice he'd left?

Furious, simply furious, Tally marched across the room, alternately balling her hands and flexing them, trying so hard to contain her temper when all she wanted to do was let out a scream.

He'd brought her so far, taken her from what she'd known, made love to her and then left. Left and left her here, behind, alone without him?

He was a beast, an absolute beast and she hated him. She did. It wasn't love she felt, it was hate. There was no way she was going to love a man who didn't talk to her, communicate with her. She refused to love a man who would just come and go and expect her to stay behind, happily waiting.

Wrong. He was wrong, wrong, wrong and considering he had an English mother and education he should know that Western women don't just wait for a man. They don't just sit around and drink tea and wait for life to come, wait for life to happen.

A flutter of pink-gold caught her eyes. The breeze was blowing through the open French doors, lifting the delicate pink-gold sheer curtains hanging inside and Tally watched the petal-pink and gold sheers swirl, the gold starbursts in the sheer curtains catching, reflecting the fading sunlight. It was beautiful, the bursts of gold and pink, beautiful in a way that filled her heart with pain.

She felt so much her chest ached. It actually ached and Tally put a hand to her mouth to hold back the sadness swamping her.

Oh, she didn't like feeling this way. Didn't like feeling left, forgotten.

Fighting tears she spun on her heel, and her silky robes flared out. Tally could feel the delicate fabric brush her bare calves but the wispy caress of fabric maddened her, just as the tender aching in her chest infuriated her. She didn't want to feel. Not if feeling hurt. Not if feeling made her feel worse.

This is why she'd left home. This is why she'd become an adventurer, explorer. Far better to risk life and limb than sit captive, passive, then sit with hurt and heartbreak.

Tally reached the wall and turned sharply to retrace her steps. Come on, Tal, she said to herself, trying to be reasonable not emotional. He won't be gone a week. He'll be back soon. He will.

But it didn't help. And it wasn't that she couldn't go two days, or even five days, without his blasted company—God knows it'd be a relief not to have to endure his sarcasm and mocking smiles—but he should have told her. He should have communicated with her. He should have told her himself.

If he'd cared, he would have.

If he cared…

Tally stopped pacing, arms going slack, heart squeezing. Maybe that was what was driving her mad. She wanted him to care. She wanted him to care and he didn't.

Oh God. It was true. He'd never said he'd cared. He'd said he wanted her. He'd said he'd possess her and claim her. He'd said many things about ownership but never once about love.

Her lower lip trembled and she bit into it ruthlessly. What did you expect, Tally girl? It's one thing to care about your neighbors, and have feelings of goodwill for those around you, and those less fortunate than you, but to fall for a Berber sheikh? For a man that would rather kidnap women than meet them on an online dating service?

Numbly Tally sat down on the carved chest in front of the window and stared blindly out at a horizon she didn't see. What she saw was herself. What she saw was heartache.

What she saw was loneliness and pain. Men like Tair didn't want to be close to other people, least of all women. Men like Tair didn't share feelings and communicate emotions, or needs or dreams. No, they made decisions. They took action. But they didn't let anyone get close. Didn't become vulnerable.

Tally knew about men like Tair because Paolo, her Brazilian lover and friend, had been the same.

And look where that got him. Dead. Falling off Everest in one of his daring adventures.

Exhaling hard, Tally blew out a stream of air, and with a shaking hand pushed a long strand of hair back from her eyes. She'd fallen so hard for him, too.

She'd fallen just the way Paolo had and just like Paolo she had no safety line, no rope or anchor. She was just going down.

Her fingers curled, her stomach knotting the same way. What had she done? What had she been thinking? How could she have let down her guard, allowed him into her heart? Hadn't she been hurt before? Hadn't Paolo's death taught her anything?

Good grief, if she was going to fall in love again, why couldn't she fall for a nice, sensitive man who'd treat her like a princess, someone who'd put *her* first?

Maybe because she wasn't comfortable with touchy-feely men. Maybe because men who kept her at arm's length made her work for their love, made her feel as if she had to earn their love. Like her father.

After all, isn't that why she'd stayed home as long as she did? Wanting to prove to her dad that she was loyal? Loving? Good?

That she—of all the kids—respected him most. Loved him best.

Tally bit her tongue, gave her head a faint shake. Couldn't be. Couldn't be. That wasn't the case, wasn't the scenario at all. She stayed home, gave up her UCLA scholarship because she was needed, not because she had to be Daddy's girl.

Goddamn it, she wasn't Daddy's girl.

She blinked, her eyes suddenly burning, her chest feeling just as hot, her throat filled with the same gritty emotion. It would have been pointless to give up her college scholarship, her chance to play volleyball at a top ranked school for her father's love. That would have been stupid. She wasn't his favorite, not even close. Mandy was his girl. And the boys, they were his, too. But not asthmatic Tally with her serious brown hair and serious brown eyes and serious tortoise frame glasses she wore until she got contact lenses her sophomore year of high school.

Serious Tally—even as a killer athlete—was never Dad's girl. Not even when she did everything exactly right.

Tally reached out, grasped a handful of the silk curtain, crushing the sheer panel in her palm. How pointless it had been to do everything right. How pointless to have given up her dreams to try to make his come true.

If only she'd been bad. If only she'd been more selfish. If only she'd learned to be tougher, harder sooner.

Her fingers tightened convulsively around the fabric, squishing it into a smaller ball of silk. Feelings weren't good. Feelings, she knew, couldn't be trusted.

Just like now.

Tally drew a deep breath, held the air bottled inside her lungs until the burning sensation left her eyes, until her throat ached for another breath, until she knew she'd gotten a handle on the tumultuous feelings.

Okay. Finally she exhaled and rose. Whatever she felt wasn't going to influence her decisions. She was still going to leave here. Still going to have the adventures she wanted, adventures for one, not two. She wasn't going to let anyone interfere with her dream for herself—least of all a desert bandit sheikh named Tair.

On the second day, eager to pass the time as well as put Tair from her mind, she agreed to visit the bath house with the ladies. She had a milk bath, which seemed odd, but the women convinced her it was good for her skin.

On the third day of Tair's absence Tally permitted the ladies to henna her hands, her wrists and the soles of feet. It was a lengthy process but it took up one day and part of the next. The women giggled as the designs took shape and Tally had to admit she liked it. It was like getting a dramatic tattoo, but this one would eventually wear off.

That third night lying in bed Tally lifted one hand up, letting the moonlight illuminate the intricate patterns on her palms. It was really beautiful and she was glad she'd had it done. Even if she hated Tair.

Smile fading, Tally finally drifted off to sleep.

Tally's mood took another dramatic turn when she woke to discover that Tair had returned in the night.

Leena, Tally's attendant, brought the news along with the breakfast tray to Tally on her patio adjacent to her room. "His lordship is back," Leena said, arranging the plate and cup and small pot of Turkish coffee. "He arrived with many men last night."

Tally's heart jumped. She felt a thrill of pleasure which quickly faded as she remembered how angry she was. She wasn't going to have this kind of relationship with a man. She wouldn't be a woman that just sat around and waited to be noticed. Waited to be remembered.

"That's nice," Tally said striving to sound indifferent even as she added sugar to her coffee. She wasn't going to get excited about his return. She wasn't. But as she carried the small cup to her lips her hand shook and the coffee was tasteless in her mouth.

Food was just as bad. Blah, bland, might as well be cotton or sawdust. And yet she forced herself to eat, forced herself to act nonchalant despite the wild beating of her heart.

She wasn't entirely surprised when his shadow stretched on her sun-drenched patio. His huge shadow seemed nearly as big as that first day she met him in El Saroush. What a huge horrible man.

She'd never love him. She wouldn't.

"Good morning," Tair greeted, pulling a chair out but not immediately sitting.

She didn't know what he expected. A kiss? A warm tender embrace? *Hmph.* He certainly wasn't getting it. "You're back," she said coolly, somehow managing to hide her flurry of hope, hurt and nerves.

The corner of his mouth tugged and he sat down. "I didn't die, no."

Tally forced herself to take another bite of her sweet roll but it was nearly impossible to get it down, swallowing suddenly a skill she hadn't mastered.

"Everything all right?" he asked, accepting a coffee from Leena.

"Just dandy."

His lashes dropped, concealing his expression but not before Tally saw the gleam in his eyes. He was laughing. At her.

She clenched her jaw, anger building. Who was he to laugh at her?

Tair suddenly looked up, into her eyes. "What's wrong? You're fit to be tied."

She was. She was having a fit if nothing else. A fit of madness for ever agreeing to go to bed with someone who had to be the most arrogant man on earth.

"You look beautiful," he added kindly. "Absolutely radiant. Have you been visiting our baths?"

She glared at him. "Yes."

"Milk baths?"

Her glare deepened. "Yes."

"That's wonderful."

"Why?"

He shrugged, and then reaching out, he took her hands in his, first one and then the other. She jumped at the touch, hot sparks shooting madly from her palm through her wrist and up her arm.

Tair turned her hands over and looking at her palms, one black eyebrow lifted.

"What?" Tally demanded, immediately defensive. She didn't know why he did that to her, didn't know why she cared what he thought. His opinion didn't matter. What he thought was of no consequence.

"Nothing," he answered but she heard the mocking note in his voice, his tone indicating that he knew something she didn't—and whatever that something was, she wouldn't like it.

"I think the women did a lovely job," she said, still sharp, still defensive.

"Yes, they did."

"It's an art form."

"Yes, it is."

"So why the smirk?"

His upper lip curled. "I'm not smirking."

"You are."

He shook his head, lips twitching.

Tally tugged on her hands but he wouldn't release her. "Tell me."

His broad shoulders shrugged and a small muscle pulled in his jaw, his lips battling the smile that wanted to be there. "It's just that the design on your hands says something."

Tally's heart dropped into her stomach and she knew, she knew, what he was going to say next and he was right—she wouldn't like it one bit.

He took her wrists in his hands, and lifted one hand up, and then the other, as if reading them. "You, *laeela*, belong to me." He lifted both her hands and turned her palms toward her. "See, it says so here."

She curled her fingers into fists. "It doesn't." But she knew it did. Knew now that was why the women giggled as they dyed her hands, and why Tair had smiled that smirking smile of his.

Tally swallowed around the lump of anger. "Show me where it says that."

With the tip of his finger he traced one of the intricate designs. "This," he said, "is the Arabic symbol for love—"

Tally flung her head back even as she tried to break free of Tair's clasp. "Love?"

He shrugged, not releasing her. "I'm just reading what it says."

Tally balled her hands so he couldn't read anymore. "I'll make sure I get this stain scrubbed off immediately."

"It'll take a couple weeks…even scrubbing hard."

"Weeks," she repeated stonily.

"Usually months."

"Months."

"It's to last for the duration of our honeymoon."

Honeymoon! "There's no honeymoon."

"Not until we're married, no. But we will have a honeymoon. It's custom—"

"I don't care if it's the damn law. But we're not having one as we're not getting married."

"We are. Sorry. The papers have all been drawn."

"Undraw them."

"Can't. It's as good as done. Give up, you won't win this one."

CHAPTER ELEVEN

"You're not serious," Tally whispered.

Tair's dark eyes narrowed "Afraid so." He paused. "Where did you think I went?" he asked mildly, leaning back, letting her go free.

Tally wasted no time dragging her chair backward, defiantly moving away. "I haven't a clue and as I'm sure it has nothing to do with me, I don't want to know."

"Actually it had everything to do with you. I went to get the Mullah from town." Tair smiled—always a dangerous sign. "The judge. He's the one that will marry us."

"And what do I get for marrying you?" she mocked.

He extended his hands. "My name. My home."

"Which I don't want."

"My protection."

"Which I don't want, either."

"But which you need." He contemplated her rebellious expression for a long pensive moment. "You seemed eager to marry me four nights ago. Why the change?"

Color surged to her cheeks as she remembered their passionate night together. Sex with him had been so intense, so explosive. "It was a mistake. A moment's madness."

"A moment's madness," he repeated thoughtfully.

"Yes. And we can't marry. I won't get married, not in these circumstances, not when we have so many differences."

"Which are?"

"Everything."

"Name one."

"Religion," she said, holding up a finger.

"Name two."

"Politics."

"Name three."

"Disparities about gender and culture."

He leaned back in his chair, eyes narrowing, jaw jutting. "So that's it?" he asked, chin lifting and in the sunlight she could see the bristles of his beard, the gleaming texture of his golden skin, the lines at his mouth and she had to fight the impulse to lean forward and kiss that mouth. Her mouth. Her man. She clenched her hands in her lap, sick at heart.

She wanted him to say the words she needed, wanted him to give her the tenderness she craved. She needed him to love her. Love her.

Tally left the table, exhaled in a rush as she crossed the small patio with its pots of jasmine and citrus. The air smelled like perfume and sunlight patterned the creamy stone pavers in shades of silver and gold.

Tair's voice followed. "This is not Seattle or Bellevue or wherever you're from. This is the desert, a different world with different laws and rules. You are mine to protect, and I will protect you, whether you want it or not."

Tally turned and took a furious, frustrated step in his direction. "You can't make me do this—"

"I can. I can even say the vows for you, make the promises. You don't even have to come to the ceremony—although it'd be nice to see you there tomorrow—and we'd still be joined as husband and wife."

"As your property."

"Let's just use the word wife."

Tally shook her head frantically. She knew he was being deliberately provocative, baiting her, tormenting her. She knew he was angry with her less than enthusiastic welcome but she wasn't going to bend and she wouldn't break. "It appalls me that you would force me to marry you. It appalls me that you'd be so barbaric and heartless."

"You're not that appalled. You know me well enough now to know that I don't say one thing and do another. If I say I've claimed you, I've claimed you and twenty-four hours apart, or seventy-two, wouldn't change anything. You are mine and tomorrow we make it legal."

He could fix this. He could make this right, or at least make it better. He knew how to soothe her, comfort. But he wouldn't. He'd be a brute. He'd be insensitive and unfeeling. "I won't marry you out of duty. If I married you, it'd only be out of love."

"And you don't love me."

Her eyes burned, her heart on fire. Did he love her? Did he feel that way for her? Was he taking her out of pride? To prove a point? To show that he'd conquered her?

"No, I don't," she choked, eyes gritty, throat sore as she tried to swallow around the lump filling it, blocking air.

Expression dark, dangerous, lethal, Tair rose from his chair. "Your right hand says you do love me."

"My right hand has been hennaed by a gaggle of giggling older women. My right hand knows not what it says—"

"I think it does."

"Well I know it does not."

He shrugged, supremely indifferent. "Then perhaps you could tell your right hand—along with your heart—that maybe it should learn to like me, if not love me, as we're about to have forever together."

"Forever."

"Eternity."

"I get the concept," she snapped, glaring at him, her pulse racing far too fast for her own good. With her heart thumping this hard she couldn't think straight, couldn't get control of her emotions, couldn't find the right words to argue. But she knew she must. She knew she couldn't let this happen, knew that if Tair said he intended to marry her tomorrow then he intended to marry her tomorrow. Even his jests were true. Everything he said, he did. Which so did not bode well.

Not for the future. Much less now.

Be logical, she ordered herself now. Say something intelligent, something that makes sense.

"Why me?" she cried, settling on the most obvious argument. "I don't like you, you don't like me, we're completely different culturally. Our values clash, our interests don't align. Why not marry a woman who wants to be with you instead of one determined to keep running away?"

"You're here."

"So are one hundred other women!"

"You need me—"

"I don't—"

"You do, but since you won't accept that argument then here's another." He walked toward her, one step and another, closing the distance with his silent catlike strides that made him king of the desert. He didn't stop walking until he stood just in front of her.

Tally had to lift her chin and look up, way up, to meet his dark eyes. Her breath caught in her throat as his gaze met hers and she felt consumed by him, consumed by a heat she couldn't explain. All she knew was that when he looked at her she felt her insides melt, felt her bones dissolve.

Like now.

Hot, so hot, and the corner of his mouth lifted and he knew the effect he had, and he loved it.

"I want you as my wife because I like the way you look." He smiled a little as if he knew how she'd take the words, appreciating how offended she'd be.

"I also like the way you kiss," he drawled. "And I very much like the way you taste."

Tally's stomach flipped. She tried to look away, but his gaze was too intense and she felt caught, trapped in his smoldering eyes, his desire there, revealed for her. He was keeping nothing hidden now.

"There are few women," he added, "that taste like you. And if I am to have a wife, I want one that I can kiss and lick and eat."

Tally's stomach flipped again, so high, so fast she shook. "You have a horrible sense of humor."

His lips pulled and white wolf teeth flashed. "None whatsoever," he agreed. His dark gaze settled on her mouth, and he cocked his head, drinking her in, making her lips feel full, swollen.

Tally's belly clenched and she knotted her hands, a silent protest at his expert seduction. It wasn't fair that he could just look at her, study her, say a few words and she'd feel this way. Feel this hot and anxious, this tight and unsatisfied, muscles snapping, pulse racing, temper flaring. It wasn't fair that he created so much tension in her and that she'd want him to relieve it. Want him to satisfy her. Appease the hunger, satiate the ache.

"You don't marry a woman just because she kisses good."

"Of course you do."

"Tair—"

"Come, think like a man. If you kiss like that, God, can you imagine what a delight you'll be in bed?" He forced her head back and his mouth descended, his lips covering her, overwhelming her, lips ruthlessly parting hers to plunder the softness and sweetness inside.

Tally grabbed at Tair's robe, clutching the fabric with every bit of her strength. She didn't want to want him, didn't want to feel like this, didn't want to give in but as he shaped her body to him, she could only feel and feel how much she craved him.

His hands slid down her body, molding her curves, lingering on her breasts before setting fire to her spine and hips. His lips found that electric spot on her neck and she felt her legs nearly buckle beneath her. But he didn't let her fall. He just took his time with her, breaking down her defenses, weakening her resolve with expert touch.

Shuddering she buried her face against his chest as his palm pressed against her pelvic bone and then down over her mound, cupping the warmth of her. He didn't press into her, but then he didn't need to. It was obvious to both of them she wanted him and for Tair that was victory enough.

"You are mine," he said, lifting his head, his dark eyes burning with the same heat and desire that filled her. "Your body knows it even if your mind refuses."

"It's a physical thing," she flashed, even as she struggled to clear her head, all her senses shaken, her legs weak.

"Fine. I'll take whatever I can get." He started to walk away but turned at the doorway. "For your information, it was a ceremonial bath you took two days ago, and the henna party yesterday? Another prewedding ritual. Here in Ouaha the bride is always painted before the ceremony." His expression hardened, features grim. "You might not want to be a bride, and might not feel like marrying me but the Mullah is here and you've been prepared."

He inclined his head once. "I'll see you in a couple of hours."

Tally sagged, clutched the wall behind her. Couple of hours? *Hours?* "We're getting married *today?*"

"Yes. Leena has your dress." His granitelike jaw shifted, upper lip curling. "It's not black, blue or white."

Tair was right. The dress, part traditional caftan and part Western evening gown, was a lovely golden beige silk trimmed in velvet green and studded with silver and jewels along the dramatic velvet neckline.

The dress wasn't snug or revealing and yet the sumptuous fabric and ornamentation made it elegant and the color suited Tally's coloring, turning her eyes a darker shade of green and heightening the cream in her complexion.

Leena wanted to do Tally's eyes and makeup, and while kohl rimmed eyes and a pale face might be tradition in Ouaha, Tally didn't want the make up. She wanted to be herself. Needed to be herself. Besides, she didn't trust her eyes not to tear and the last thing she wanted was streaks of black on her cheeks.

Wrists laden with wide gold bracelets, and a gold head-piece that held a pale ivory silk veil, Tally was led to the formal reception room downstairs in the main building.

She sat while Tair and the Mullah discussed the marriage contract. Finally it was time to begin the actual exchanging of the vows.

The Mullah looked at Tair. "Are you Zein Hassim el-Tayer?"

"I am," Tair answered.

The Mullah turned now to Tally. "Are you Talitha Elizabeth Devers?" he asked slowly in broken English.

"No."

"She is, your Honor," Tair answered, giving Tally a sharp look.

"I'm not, your Honor," she answered giving Tair an equally disapproving look. "My name isn't Talitha, it's Tallis. Tallis Elizabeth Devers." She looked back at Tair, her eyebrows lifting as if to say, *so there.*

The Mullah didn't look pleased with the interruption but continued on with the ceremony. "Are you, Tallis Elizabeth Devers, being coerced into this marriage?" his voice was stern as he fixed Tally with his hard gaze.

"Yes," she answered at the same moment Tair spoke.

"No," Tair said.

The Mullah looked up from his paperwork, his reading glasses low on his nose.

"Yes," Tally repeated.

"Sheikh el-Tayer?" The Mullah asked Tair for clarification.

"No," Tair answered. "She said no, she's not."

"No," Tally said, frustration growing. "I didn't say no—"

"So it's no?" the Mullah said, looking at Tally now.

"Yes, it's no—" she broke off, shook her head. "What are you asking?"

"Do you wish to marry Sheikh Zein el-Tayer? Or are you being coerced?"

Color stormed her cheeks. "Yes."

"Yes, you want to marry him."

"Yes, I'm being coerced."

"Good. You wish to marry him. Yes." The Mullah nodded, shuffled his paperwork. "Let it be done."

And that was that. It was done. Tally had become Sheikh Tair's wife.

There was a huge celebratory party afterward, a banquet of gigantic proportions but Tally didn't have the heart—much less stomach—to eat, especially not after Tair told her they'd sit in separate sections during the banquet and celebrations.

Sit in separate sections? He still didn't get who she was, still didn't understand that he'd swept her into something so alien from her world that she still felt dizzy. Not just dizzy, but scared.

How could she live here, like this? Yes, she loved him but she didn't understand him or his culture. She wanted the hearth and home she knew growing up. Not exclusion. Not seclusion.

As the crowd surged around them after the ceremony, the men pulling Tair one way and the women pulling her another, Tally managed to slip away, leaving the banquet to run up the stairs for the sanctuary of her own room.

Fighting tears, she hiked up her long dress, tucking it into the waistband of her skirt and paced. Trapped, that's what she was. Trapped.

There was nowhere for her to go. No one to help her. She was truly alone.

And standing on her terrace, tears in her eyes, she heard the music rise from below, the one-string rababa violin mixing with the dalouka, or big drums.

Soon there would be singing and dancing. Tair had said his men, armed with swords and whips, would perform the war dance called the Al Ardha.

Tears falling, Tally looked out over the desert with its sand and more sand. How could she feel so much and none of it be easy? How could she love and still be unhappy? Where was the comfort? Where was the peace?

"What have you done to your gown?" Tair's quiet voice sounded behind her.

Tally dashed away the tears, lifted her shoulders in a shrug.

"Your legs are bare," he said.

She heard the disapproval in his voice and his censure just made the hurt worse, the wound deeper, the need for freedom more fierce.

Tally leaned forward to smell one of the miniature orange trees in one of the patio's glazed pots. "You said I could dress as I liked in private."

"Yes, in private, but this isn't private. It's a garden where many in my household could see you."

"Your household is all downstairs celebrating."

"Pull your gown down," he said sharply, losing patience.

Tally turned from the small tree. It galled her that this was her wedding day and she met his gaze directly without flinching. "No." And she forced a small competitive smile. "Thank you."

He showed his white teeth. "Please."

"I like my gown this way. I feel freer. Lighter."

"More exposed."

Tally felt a glimmer of a smile in her eyes. "Exactly."

"It's not proper."

"I don't really care about proper."

"You are my wife."

"Under protest."

"But nonetheless, my wife."

"I wish you wouldn't keep repeating yourself."

"And I wish you'd do as you're told."

Fire and fury in her heart, Tally looked at him, held his gaze, and as he watched, she deliberately yanked her skirts ever higher. Her right eyebrow arched as if to say, what now?

A small muscle pulled in his cheek. "Do you really want to fight?"

"I want you to accept that I'm not, nor ever will be, the kind of woman you want as a wife."

"It's too late to get out of the marriage. It's done. We're husband and wife. And as my wife, you must please me."

Her left eyebrow rose. "I think you've got the wrong woman, Tair."

"It's your duty, wife."

Tally walked toward him and once she'd reached him, she lifted her face to his and she took her skirts in both hands and pulled them even higher.

In the back of her mind she knew this was silly and she was behaving foolishly. She knew the issue was ridiculous and her behavior childish but Tair's arrogant high-handed manner made her see red. Everything he asked of her, everything he demanded went against her sense of self, grating her self-respect. She'd pushed herself to become her own person, to forge her own identity separate from anyone else and yet what he asked of her—demanded—seemed to negate that person.

"Tair, you might have married me, but you didn't buy me. You don't own me and can't control me. I don't have to wear your clothes the way you want me to. I can wear clothes the way I want just as I can keep my own name, my own personality, my own identity."

"You're not going to win, wife."

"But I'm sure going to fight, husband."

Tair leaned forward, closing the distance between them but instead of reaching for her with his hands he lowered his head little by little until his mouth was just inches from her.

He didn't move again, just stood there, his lips nearly

touching hers, and she felt her muscles tighten, her stomach squeezing, air bottling in her lungs.

She could smell the subtle spicy fragrance he wore, and feel the warmth of his skin and she remembered far too well how his mouth felt on hers, how her lower back prickled and her heart raced and the intense pleasure pain.

"You should have married a Berber girl," she whispered, trying to ignore the hot and cold ripples beneath her skin and the fierce coil of desire in her belly. She didn't have to have him. She didn't need to be touched by him. She didn't want anything he had to offer.

She didn't.

Then his head dropped and he closed the distance, and covered her lips with his.

White-hot lightning whipped through her. Her eyes fluttered closed and she sucked in air as her pulse quickened then slowed.

God, he was horrible. The kiss was so light, so gentle, so persuasive that she found herself leaning toward him, wanting more. He knew already how she liked to be kissed.

Take me, she thought. Take me here.

Tair lifted his head, dark eyes knowing, aware. "Come with me," he said, and kissing her once more he tugged her skirts down until all the fabric fell in long elegant folds covering her legs. "Tonight we shall finish this fight, but now, wife, isn't the time."

But that night after all the guests had gone and Tair had swept Tally in his arms and carried her to his bed, she didn't want to fight. She just wanted him—heart, mind, body and soul.

Their lovemaking was far from tender. Tair took her, possessed her, with a carnal intensity and Tally responded with the same fierce hunger. He made her furious and yet he also made her burn and hurt, wanting him, needing him, needing to be loved by him.

His fingers locked with hers and he held her arms over her

head as his body surged into her, his hips relentlessly driving and yet she wanted it, wanted him, and wrapping her legs around his waist she welcomed his body, welcomed the wild passion of him.

She fell asleep in his arms, damp, exhausted, and only partly satisfied. Her dreams were vivid and intense, dreams of women singing and drums beating and the heavy sweet smell of attar, the uniquely Arabic perfume she'd first smelled in Atiq and now here. And then in her dreams shrouded men with swords and whips stormed her room, taking Tair, dragging Tair far from her.

Tally woke with a start, heart racing, hands flying out to brace a fall.

But she wasn't falling. She was still in bed.

She reached out to touch the bed and instead her palm brushed warm skin and solid muscle. And heart still pounding she remembered. She was still here, at Bur Juman with Tair.

With Tair.

Putting her head back down, she left her hand on his chest and looked at him in the dark for a long moment, emotions fierce, intense, everything breaking loose. Everything stronger than she ever thought she'd know, feel. She loved him. The horrible man. Her horrible man. And she loved him more than she thought she could ever love anyone.

Tally's lashes slowly drifted down, and she exhaled softly, painfully. She was still here with Tair.

Thank God.

CHAPTER TWELVE

It was the morning after the wedding and Tair was of course nowhere to be found while Leena was in Tally's bedroom with her putting away all the new clothes Tair had ordered for his new bride.

Leena was very excited about Tally's new wardrobe but Tally could hardly bring herself to look at the myriad of new gowns and robes. Instead she stood at the window, looking out at the desert and wanting to go, just go. Not to necessarily leave Tair, but to leave here, leave the confinement and the women's quarters and the world that kept her in long dresses and veils and away from action. Adventure.

She missed action and adventure. Wistfully she looked at the sand dunes and the shimmer of sun on the undulating hills.

From here, the room in her tower, the sand was beautiful. Mystical. From here, she even missed the sandstorm and sand pit and her asthma attack.

Tair had saved her each time. He'd come to the rescue, riding hard and fast on his white and gray stallion. He'd saved her.

Tally bit her lip, trying to ignore the ache in her chest. The ache was different from yesterday's anger. Her dream last night had frightened her, made her realize how little control she had. Not just over Tair, but Paolo, her family, her father. Life was slippery, nearly as slippery as those grains of quicksand.

"I like you, Madame," Leena said unexpectedly.

Tally turned from the window, smiled. She was touched. "I like you, too. You're very good to me. I appreciate it."

Leena smoothed one of the gorgeous silk sheaths that rested on her lap. She'd been putting each gown carefully into the enormous carved trunk. "I wish I could be like you. Fierce and brave. Strong."

Tally pushed a heavily jeweled hand through her hair, the myriad of gold bangles on her wrist jingling. "I'm not that brave," she answered, moving to sit on the edge of her bed. No, she wasn't brave. She actually felt like a coward. She felt afraid. Afraid for her, afraid for Tair. It was only a dream—not a foreshadowing—but it unnerved her, leaving her tender on the inside, tender and fragile. "I think I just like fighting with his lordship."

The girl's smile dimpled from behind the sheer veil. "Because you love him."

"I don't love him."

"He loves you."

"He doesn't."

The girl shrugged. "Then why does he permit you to speak to him as you do? No one else could address Sheikh el-Tayer that way. But when you open your mouth, he listens."

"Maybe it's because I'm Western."

"He's had other foreign women and he's not allowed any of them to speak to him as you do."

Tally's eyes widened. What did Leena mean, other Western women here? But she wasn't going to ask, couldn't ask Leena, wasn't right. But Tally couldn't stay quiet. "He used to entertain here frequently?"

"Not entertain, no, but there have been…" And Leena's voice drifted off and her shoulders shrugged. "Not a harem, no, but you must understand, he is a sheikh and he has had many women."

"*Western* women?"

"French. British." Leena's forehead furrowed. "One Canadian."

Tally nearly slipped off the bed. "They were here?"

"Yes, Madame."

"And they left?" Tally pressed her knuckles against the silk coverlet on the bed. "The Sheikh allowed them to leave?"

"Of course, Madame." Leena looked at her uncertainly. "But why wouldn't he?"

"I'm just going to have a word with my husband the Sheikh."

"And your husband is here." Tair gestured to Leena that she should go. He waited for the door to close. "What do you need to speak to me about?"

Tally sat on the bed and looked up at her husband, a man that towered over other men, a man with huge shoulders and a chiseled jaw and a stomach that was nothing but a ripple of hard, carved muscle.

This man was her husband. This man. A *sheikh*. And so what did that make her?

She stared at him so long and hard it hurt. If she was Tair's woman what did it make her? And then it hit her.

She was the Sheikh's captive bride.

Tally nearly smiled at the wretched state of affairs. One day into her marriage and she was already lost. How on earth was this going to work?

"What did you want to ask me, Woman?" Tair's deep voice cut through her fog of misery.

She chewed on her inner lip trying to think of a way to ask him about what Leena had told her without divulging that it was Leena who had told her. Tally didn't want Leena punished for gossiping. And maybe it was only gossip. Maybe Leena didn't really know the truth…maybe it wasn't the way it seemed…

"You've had other women here, at Bur Juman." Tally's gaze searched his autocratic face with its regal brow and nose and the jaw that could only belong to a man like Tair. Hard, fixed, immobile. "Is that true?"

He hesitated, and his gaze examined her just as closely as she'd studied him. "I could play dumb."

"You could."

"But I won't insult your intelligence."

"Thank you."

"There have been other women here."

Tally swallowed, surprised at how much it hurt, the idea of Tair with other women. Of course he had to have had other women. He knew exactly what to do with a woman—at least in the bedroom—and while part of his skill might be natural talent, the rest of it…the timing, the ability to hold back, the knowledge of a woman's most sensitive zones…that was education. "European women? Americans? Canadians?"

The corner of his mouth tugged but he wasn't smiling. "Someone's been talking."

"And they all were your lovers?"

His dark head inclined and his gaze narrowed, creases fanning from his eyes. He suddenly looked wise, and weary. "Yes."

"Where are they now?"

"Gone."

"Dead?"

He laughed shortly, not at all amused. "I've never hurt a woman. I'm a man, maybe not honorable, but not violent with women."

She nearly rolled her eyes. "So you let them leave after they visited you here?"

"Of course."

Of course. She felt her own lips curve, a tremulous smile of recognition that she'd caught him in a lie. A deliberate mistruth, one that had allowed him to manipulate her. Trap her. Her insides knotted, cramping. "You told me I couldn't leave here, you said I knew too much about your life, that I carried all the pictures in my head…" Her voice drifted off and she just looked at him, waiting for the explanation or apology, for the facts that would clear this horrible misunderstanding up.

Let him be heroic. Let him be good. Let him be true. At least, true to her.

Let him care enough about her to do what was best for her.

But Tair didn't answer and appeared indifferent. Blasé.

Why had she even begun this? Why care about the truth, whatever the truth was? She searched his dark eyes again. "You didn't have to keep me here, did you?"

For a minute she didn't think he was going to answer. She thought he'd pull the silent routine but he surprised her by smiling faintly. "No," he said. "I didn't have to keep you here. I could have let you go. I just didn't want you to."

"You lied to me."

"Tricked you, too."

She shook her head sadly, hurt, so hurt she could barely keep her heartbreak from showing. "Why?"

"All's fair in love and war."

"And you're a man of war," she said bitterly. "Soussi el-Kebir."

His expression was mocking. "The big man of the desert."

Tally rose, headed for the patio, needing air, space, relief. As she headed through the arched doorway Tair's voice followed her.

"Has Leena packed your travel bag? We leave for our honeymoon in the next hour."

"Honeymoon? You've got to be joking. I don't want to go anywhere with you."

"I know. But the plans have already been made and I'm not about to disappoint my mother."

Tally turned to face him. "We're going to Atiq?"

"My mother is anxious to meet my new wife."

"Does she know you forced me into marriage? Does she know that you kidnapped me and lied to me and tricked me into being your wife?"

Tair's jaw shifted. "Yes."

"And what did she say?"

Deep grooves formed on either side of his mouth. "That I'm just like my father."

An hour later they'd left the walled safety of Bur Juman behind riding on horseback for the distant city of Atiq. It would be a two-day journey. Tonight they'd overnight close to the border then in the morning switch the horses for four-wheel drive vehicles. At midday after they reached Fez, they'd leave the cars for Tair's private jet.

Living in such a rugged, untouched part of the world had its pluses, as well as minuses and it was only when Tair needed to make the trip to Baraka's·capital city that the remoteness of Ouaha troubled him.

As they rode, Tair kept a close eye on Tally, making sure her horse never slowed or wandered. He knew his men were riding on all sides but he wouldn't take any chances with her safety. Or her state of mind.

She was angry, very angry and he didn't blame her. Everything she'd said was true. Everything he'd done had been manipulative. The problem was, in her world what he'd done was wrong. Immoral. But in his world, he'd been sly, clever. He'd found the woman he wanted and taken her, made her his. In his world this was good. Successful.

She was right about their worlds being different and he at least had the advantage of knowing her world having a mother who was English and years in English boarding school. Now his mother had never returned to England after marrying his father—another successful kidnapping story—but she was also a spirited woman, beautiful, educated, proud.

Tair's first wife, Ara, was Barakan—a chieftain's daughter—but she and Tair's mother were like two peas in a pod. They'd been close, Ara becoming the daughter his mother never had. Then the slaughter in the desert and all their lives changed.

It was then his mother moved to Atiq, giving up her beloved Bur Juman for the relative safety—and anonymity—of Baraka's largest city.

She lived close to the Nuri's palace, in a compound of her own but with excellent security. The Sultan Malik Nuri and his wife Nicolette included Tair's mother in many government and social events. Between her teaching and her friends at the palace, his mother lived a full life. But he knew his mother missed Ara and desperately grieved for the grandchild she lost. Zaki had been her only grandchild and it was hard on his mother—a good, kind and loving woman—to have lost so many of those she loved.

Tair hoped Tally would like his mother. He knew his mother would love Tally. He also knew that his mother hoped for more grandchildren.

Tair glanced at Tally who rode not far from him, her back tall, head high, eyes straight forward. She was so furious with him, barely speaking to him, answering in monosyllables.

That would change once he had her alone later, in his bed. She'd be far warmer and more eager to talk then.

They reached El Saroush just before nightfall and Tally gave his men orders. Some were to inspect the city palace maintained by the el-Tayer family for the past two hundred years. Others were to see to the horses. Others were to keep watch during the first part of the night.

Tair showed Tally where her room would be and told her that dinner would be served shortly. He encouraged her to explore the interior gardens where the purple and mauve jacarandas were in full bloom but not to leave the palace's high walls and impenetrable iron gates.

Tally was happy to wander through the walled courtyards and fragrant gardens. After riding all day she was tired and sore and she found the gardens, now illuminated at night by ancient torches, beautiful as well as inviting.

The assault happened so fast Tally wasn't even sure what had happened until it was all over. In one of the gardens she'd bent over a fountain to see the intricate mosaic in the bottom of the pool when a man grabbed her from behind, covered her mouth and nose and pressed something sharp against her ribs.

It was like the morning she'd been kidnapped by Tair—one moment she was fine, intent on taking pictures, and the next she was in danger. She bit the hand covering her mouth only to be rewarded with a forearm against her throat, pressing tight.

"You make a sound and you will die," a rough voice muttered in her ear. "Understand?"

He spoke English, excellent English. In fact, she recognized the voice and accent. "Sadiq?" she asked, realizing it was her translator. The man who'd spent two weeks with her traveling from Atiq to El Saroush.

"Be quiet and you won't get hurt," he said.

Tally nodded, wincing as the knife blade was pressed harder against her side. She could feel it nick, cut, but she wasn't afraid, not as afraid as she should be. Tair had said the men she'd traveled with were Barakan rebels, zealots who refused to recognize Ouaha as an independent territory. *"Ash bhiti?* What do you want?" she whispered, speaking the simple Arabic she'd learned, and calmed by the knowledge that Tair would help her. Tair would save her. He always did.

"How many are with him?"

"With who?" she asked, deliberately playing dumb because she knew this was about Tair. It had to be about Tair.

The forearm against her throat tightened, bruising. "Don't be stupid."

She wouldn't tell him anything. "I'm afraid I don't understand."

Her captor didn't like her response and he increased the pressure on her throat, ruthlessly punishing, squeezing, cutting off her air. Tally's head swam. Little spots danced before her eyes and just as her knees started to buckle everything went dark.

When Tally came round she was no longer in the palace garden by the fountain and pool. She was in a plain room somewhere, hands and feet tied, tethered to a chair. It was dark in the room and even though the shutters at the windows were closed, she knew it had to be dark outside. In the desert sunlight always penetrated the shutters and blinds but the room was eerily dark, almost black, and Tally felt fear. But also calm.

Tair would come. Tair would find her. Tair would save her before it was too late.

It was a long night but she did sleep for a while and when she woke again light outlined the square windows and poked through cracks and holes in the weathered wood shutters.

Tally glanced around the room and discovered she wasn't alone, either.

"So you're awake," the man said.

It was a different man than last night, and blinking Tally stared at him, wondering where the other one had gone, wondering what would happen next.

"How is your throat?" the man asked. "Sore?"

She swallowed, her gaze holding his and nodded.

"Sadiq wasn't to hurt you. He's been punished."

Tally just continued to hold his gaze and looking at him, she made a point of pulling on her hands, showing him she was tied, showing him she didn't like it.

"It's for your safety," he said almost apologetically. "This way you will be protected."

"From whom?" Tally finally spoke, her voice, rough, bruised, but her words were bitter and they betrayed her anger. "I certainly wouldn't hurt myself. So who would hurt me?"

He didn't answer her question, he merely shrugged and offered her an affable smile. "I am Imran. I want to help you." He extended his hands, demonstrating his friendliness, trustworthiness. "Tell me where you want to go. I will personally see you there."

"Tell me what you want first."

"Details about Sheikh el-Tayer's home. His travels. Future plans." Imran paused. "Things of that nature."

"I don't know any of that. He doesn't talk to me—"

"You're his wife, aren't you?"

"Yes but he's Sheikh el-Tayer. He doesn't confide in women."

Imran regarded her steadily, his gaze unwavering. "We just want him. We don't want to hurt you."

But they would hurt her. They'd do anything they could to get to Tair.

Tair was in trouble.

And she, somehow, unwittingly, was going to make it worse for him. Because she knew Tair and he would come after her. He wouldn't leave her, not behind, not even to save himself. Her Tair would risk himself to save her.

And she had to do the same. Something to help Tair, to protect him. "And if I help you, you'll send me home? You'll let me go?"

Imran smiled. "I'll take you to the airport myself," he answered.

Yes, she thought, in a body bag. Because now she knew just who and what she was dealing with. And Tair had been right. They were lawless men. Men who'd do anything to further their cause.

"We're returning to the desert late tomorrow," she said. "Going back to his home at Bur Juman."

"You know the way there?"

"But of course. I've spent the past few weeks there."

"You can show us?"

"Yes."

"I hope so. Because if anything goes wrong, if you're trying to be clever, you'll pay. We'll make you suffer."

Tair took a deep, sharp breath, lungs expanding to allow the searing blade of pain to slice between his ribs, up toward his heart. Up to his ugly blackened, badly scarred heart.

He was livid. Beyond livid. He was close to violence.

His men hadn't protected the palace or Tally. His men had fallen asleep on the job. Just as he had.

It killed him. Tally kidnapped. Taken. And he not being prepared. He felt worse than an amateur. He felt like a failure.

But he knew where she was, he knew who had taken her, knew that Tally's hired escort had been working in conjunction with Ashraf who had poisoned her.

It was hard to trust anyone. Much less himself.

Remorse and recriminations would have to wait. He could inflict his damage later. First he needed Tally safe.

In the house where Tally was being held hostage, the door to the upstairs bedroom suddenly burst open and Tair was there, scooping her into his arms.

"Hania?" he asked, cutting the robes that bound her hands and feet. *Are you well?*

She nodded, slumped a little with fatigue against his chest, gulping in great breaths of air. As Tair walked out of the chamber she spotted a crumpled body in the hallway next to her door. She shuddered and looked away, not wanting to know if he was alive or dead, not wanting anything but to leave this godforsaken place.

Her arm wrapped around his neck. "I didn't hear you outside."

"I am very quiet."

"Thank you."

He made a rough inarticulate sound that she didn't understand but she felt his chest vibrate and his hold on her tightened.

She knew he'd protect her. He'd protect her no matter what.

He loves me in his way, she thought. He loves me the way he knows how and it was enough. "I knew you'd come," she whispered, a lump forming in her throat.

"Did you?"

She nodded, insides knotting, emotions strange and strained. She never wanted to care for him; never expected him to care for her. Love between two people such as they complicated everything. It wasn't the tidy romantic love of Western culture—the love captured in movies and popular bestsellers. Love here in the desert was hard, fierce, sacrificial.

Love here wasn't safe. Love in Ouaha was dangerous, nearly as dangerous as Tair himself.

"Put me down," she said as they reached the street and were circled by Tair's men. "I can walk."

Tair put Tally down, let her walk.

They were in trouble. *He* was in trouble. He couldn't do this. Couldn't make this work. Not like this, not when he felt the way he did these past forty-eight hours, the worst hours he'd known since discovering the slaughtered bodies of his wife and tiny son. Feeling what he'd felt, going where he'd gone—into an endless abyss, a place of such darkness that he could only describe it as absolute rage and despair—and it wasn't a place he could handle, wasn't a place that allowed him to be.

He couldn't be *Soussi el-Kebir,* or Sheikh el-Tayer, not with Tally here.

The marauding Barakan rebels were cowards and villains and they didn't just pillage and burn. They'd slaughtered the elderly, the women, the children. Ara and Zaki had been among the dead in the terrible bloodbath seven years ago. But seven years seemed like nothing when he remembered his terror as he returned from Atiq riding through the night, riding with heaven and hell in his heart, only to arrive home and hold his five-year-old as Zaki died.

Tair wouldn't let himself think much more than that.

But he knew, he knew in his black scarred heart, that he couldn't go through that loss again, and he couldn't think, lead, guide—not with Tally here. It was one thing to have a mistress. Another to have a beloved wife.

And Tally was his—she'd been his from the start—and she made him afraid, made him worry, made him a man.

But he couldn't risk being an ordinary man. Mortal. He had to remain a monster. Frankenstein-like in his inability to give, or feel.

Tally. His woman.

He'd have to send her back, send her home. Not to his home, but hers, that loft space she rented in downtown Seattle's historic district.

He felt Tally slip her hand into his as they approached the waiting armored cars. His jaw hardened and he didn't look at her, didn't let himself think or feel. Once his mind was made up, he never changed it.

There'd be no reasoning with him, no pleading or emotional protests. He'd seen too much, known too much, lost too much to be moved by talk or tears.

He'd already battled death, grief, sorrow on his own and it'd taught him that strength came from loss. Power came from fear. Courage from the absence of hope.

A woman's tears didn't move him. Not if it meant he'd save her life. If not his own.

CHAPTER THIRTEEN

"TAIR," Tally whispered.

His fingers tightened around hers. *"Iya?"* Yes.

There was a brief pause. "Are you mad at me?"

"La." No.

"Okay."

But Tally wasn't reassured and as they passed through Tair's men, armed with swords and guns to enter the four-wheel drive vehicle, Tally flashed back to the dream she'd had on her wedding night. The dream of the robed men carrying swords and whips and how they'd taken Tair from her.

But Tair wasn't gone, she reminded herself as the doors closed and Tair personally locked them. Tair was here. Everything would be fine.

But on the way to Fez nothing was fine. For the first hour Tair barely looked at her and didn't speak. Tally looked at Tair and worried.

He could say that he wasn't angry with her, but he was definitely upset. "I'm sorry," she finally ventured. "I'm sorry about what happened—"

"It's not your fault."

But somehow she knew it was. She knew they'd used her to try to get to Tair and she knew Tair had had to come rescue her. Again. "I wasn't going to take them to Bur Juman. I wouldn't have—"

"They kill women, Tally."

Tally bit her tongue, waited for whatever else it was that Tair had to say. But what she thought he'd say and what he did say were two different things.

"This isn't working." His voice was hard and sharp. It was the voice of a stranger. "It's time for you to return to America."

Blood surged to her cheeks—hurt, shock, humiliation but she didn't flinch, not outwardly. "I don't understand."

His dark gaze was eerily cold, hard, ice in the desert as he stared into her eyes. "Then listen to me. I'm telling you. I don't want you here."

"Here." She pounced on the word as if it were the rope that Tair had thrown her the day she was sinking in the sand pit. "You don't want me here. But you do want me."

"No." His expression grew harder if it were possible, the dark eyes crackling with ice and storm. "I don't want you. I've—" and he took a quick fast breath "—tired of you."

Tally's upper lip twitched, an involuntary reflex. Pain. Panic. Disbelief. He didn't mean it. He couldn't mean it. She was his. *She was his.* She'd been his since that first day in the desert… "Tair." Her voice was but a whisper, husky, pleading.

"I will see you to Atiq. Make sure you board the correct flight. We go today."

"Today?" Her head was spinning. She couldn't follow him, couldn't see how she'd gone from a night in his bed, an endless night of endless exquisite lovemaking. A night without words, a night of just touch, a night where the caress of his fingers and lips meant more than words ever could and yet now…now…

"Tair." Tally couldn't even look at him, couldn't bear to see so much ice and disdain in his eyes, not in those beautiful eyes she loved, not in that fierce face of his that had always gentled when he looked at her. But it wasn't gentling now. There was nothing gentle about him anymore.

But Tally wasn't ready to quit. She didn't know how to quit, hadn't perfected giving up. "I don't believe you. I don't. You're just mad about something. I must have done something—"

"No, Tally, it's not something you've done. It's me. This is about me. I'm…bored."

Bored.

Tally nearly choked, air strangling in her throat. Her face felt strange. Her skin hot, so hot it was going to peel off her face. "I've never bored you," she retorted fiercely. "Never."

"Well, I'm bored now."

"You're not. Maybe you realized you couldn't handle me. Maybe that's what you're feeling, but it's not boredom."

He stared at her with cold, dead eyes. "You can protest all you want, but I know what I want, know what I feel—"

"You, feel? When did you start to feel?"

"—and I'm done. Finished. I need something else. Something you can't give."

It was like a knife in her chest, plunging through her breast-bone into her lungs. She couldn't breathe, couldn't get air, couldn't get anything in or out of her chest. It felt like he was killing her, destroying her. Acid tears sprung to her eyes and her throat ached, as she took a step backward and then another. "You were the one that insisted we marry. You were the one that pushed. You—"

"I was impulsive. Wrong. The marriage will be annulled."

"Annulled."

"It will take some paperwork, maybe some money chang-ing hands, but within a few weeks you will be single again."

She reached for the ornate trunk in Tair's room to steady herself, needing something to give her courage. Strength. "You can say that, but we made vows. Promises. Promises I fully intend to keep."

"You're not in America. This isn't Hollywood," he contin-ued coldly, ruthlessly, "this doesn't have a happy ending. This is life. Reality. I was wrong to think you could live here, be here. I was wrong to think you were the right woman for me.

You're too different. Too—" and he broke off, searching for the right word, "Difficult."

Tally just looked at him, unable to find words or her voice.

"I don't want everything to be a fight," he continued mercilessly. "I have men to fight with. You don't behave like a woman. Instead of letting me be the master, you're always trying to take over, take charge and I'm tired of it. Bored. Better to end it now before things get complicated." He nodded at her flat belly, knowing she'd just had her period, knowing she wasn't pregnant and obviously not wanting to take another chance. "Pack whatever you need. Your cameras and memory cards will of course be returned to you."

That afternoon they traveled in silence through the crowded streets, past small neighborhoods and walled estates, palm trees shocking green against whitewashed buildings and the cobalt blue sky.

Arriving at the private airport used exclusively by royalty and the wealthiest of the wealthy, Tair walked Tally from the limousine to the jet on the tarmac.

He moved to take her elbow to help her up the stairs but Tally shook him off. If he was sending her away he didn't need to be so damn helpful.

He entered the jet with her, checked to make sure everything was okay before putting her small knapsack on the cream and red wool carpet.

Fighting tears, Tally stared at the carpet, thinking even her khaki knapsack looked forlorn.

"You'll be home before you know it," Tair said. "Soon this will just seem like a bad dream."

She shook her head. She couldn't speak, couldn't make a single sound.

Tair leaned forward to kiss her goodbye but she stepped back, moving away. If he didn't want her, he couldn't kiss her, either.

"It just wasn't mean to be," he said.

"You don't love me?" she asked, finally finding the words even though they were horrible to say.

He was silent and then the answer came. "No."

Tally turned away so she wouldn't have to watch him leave. But as the airplane door closed Tally felt as if her heart was being ripped apart.

He didn't love her.

Four words, four little words but words with the power to cut. Crush. Break her.

Like he just did.

Tally couldn't even cry, not then, not during the flight that went on and on. Not while the taxi took her from Boeing Field's executive airport home. Not while she struggled to unlock the door of her apartment.

But once the door shut, once she turned on the lights and looked around the place she hadn't been in nearly six months her control shattered.

He didn't love her. He'd never loved her. It was just a bad mistake.

The first week she was back she didn't think, couldn't think, couldn't even function. Tally spent more time in bed than out of it. More time with her face buried in her pillow crying her eyes out than functioning like a normal human being but she couldn't function. Couldn't eat. Couldn't sleep. Could only cry as if her heart were breaking. And it was breaking. It was shattering into little pieces of nothing.

He was horrible, hateful. How could he have sent her home like this?

How could he care so little that he'd just toss her aside? Throw her away as though she were garbage. Refuse.

It'd been so long since she'd been rejected like this, so long since she'd felt so bad about herself.

She thought he had cared. Maybe not deeply, forever love, but enough. Enough. Enough to keep her, love her, make her his.

Stop this, she told herself, stop thinking, feeling—just stop.

Eyes swollen from crying, Tally rolled from bed, desperate to put an end to the hurt, and the tears, and the heartbreak.

Despite her misery, she forced herself out to buy groceries. A day later she made herself watch a movie on cable television. On the weekend she went for a walk despite the black clouds overhead, walking for hours through rain; along the wharf and the piers where the ferries arrived and departed, silently sailing like giant wedding cakes on the dramatic Puget Sound. She walked to keep the tears from coming and it worked. As long as she kept moving, she was fine.

Ten days after returning she picked up her camera and went out to shoot whatever inspiration came.

But then on day seventeen Tally developed her memory cards of film and flipped through a couple hundred shots before coming across the last picture she took in Ouaha. It was the shot from the medina, near the well when the gunfire rang out and everyone ducked and covered as Tair and his men rode like hell's fire down the streets, taking Tally with them.

Tally studied the print for a long moment, seeing the children she'd been focusing on and yet there in the background was a horse pawing the air.

Tair.

Tair.

And just like that she was back in Ouaha, back in his home of sand and stone, back with the endless nights and the blistering heat.

Tally closed her eyes, and crumpled the photo in her hand. She wouldn't remember. Wouldn't go there. And instead of letting herself remember anymore, she e-mailed her editor and the senior editor she worked with letting them know she had prints she'd be sending. And then she got into her darkroom and began developing her black and white shots the old-fashioned way, taking time with processing, blowing up some shots, cropping others, printing on the special thick acid free paper she favored.

Her editors e-mailed her back promptly. They wanted to

see the pictures. They were eager to see where she'd gone, what she'd been doing these past four months in Northern Africa and the Middle East.

Tally buried herself in work, finding solace in long hours and a devotion to her art. It was at night, and on the weekends, that the lost sensation returned, that feeling she'd been drawn and quartered. Disemboweled.

It was at night and on weekends she didn't know what to do with herself, at night and weekends when she found it strange being home. After nearly a year on the road she realized she'd become a true nomad. She knew she'd had an apartment but forgot what it looked like, felt like, and for those first two months back in Seattle she felt like a stranger in her own place.

It wasn't even Seattle that felt so strange. It was—and Tally couldn't believe this—being alone.

Alone. She, the girl who'd decided she preferred being alone, didn't like being alone anymore.

Tair had done this to her. Tair. But that didn't mean she had to cry over him anymore. She was done crying, done grieving. She'd wasted too much time as it was on a man who didn't love her. Wouldn't love her.

Tally was just about to head out to photograph Alki Beach when a courier arrived with a package from Baraka. She sat on the bottom step of her staircase to open the brown padded envelope. And then the velvet box inside.

Emerald fire glinted at her. It was an emerald and diamond necklace, the kind of necklace only royalty and celebrities could wear. There was a small card nestled in the white satin lining. Tair.

Tair. Terrible, horrible hateful Tair.

Hands shaking, Tally snapped the lid down. Thanks, Tair, but no thanks. She wasn't going to be keeping this.

There was just one problem. No one would take the necklace back. With its twelve plus carats of diamonds and emeralds and the delicate platinum setting, no insurance company wanted to touch a necklace that was valued at over a quarter million dollars. Especially as the Sheikh's address was the middle of the Sahara desert.

And suddenly Tally was angry all over again. Instead of blocking out the memories, they all came rushing back, one after the other and they didn't fade. She remembered it all, remembered everything. The kidnapping from town. The asthma attack. The sandstorm. The quicksand. The knife. The poison.

Then Bur Juman and the first night they made love.

Tally swallowed hard around the lump filling her throat. She wasn't going to cry. She wouldn't cry.

But oh those battles.

She'd thought in the beginning that she'd hate him forever, thought she'd never like him, much less understand him, but that had changed. How that had changed…

Tally sank into the cushions of her couch, the old suede sofa more comfortable than attractive and the cushions gave way, swallowing her up even as she brushed away a stray tear.

To hell with him. She didn't need him. She didn't need another person in her life that didn't want her, or appreciate her. She'd spent way too many years throwing herself away, not valuing herself. She wouldn't do it again. Not anymore. Which is why she wouldn't cry for herself, or feel sorry for herself, or have one single regret much less one sad thought. He wasn't worth it.

He wasn't.

Not even if he was her husband and the horrible man she'd fallen in love with.

Tally grabbed a pillow and punched it and punched again. If only he wasn't so impossible.

And so good-looking.

And smart.

And amazing in bed.

Howling her frustration, Tally threw the pillow up, up at

the industrial ceiling shot with massive metal trusses and beams. "I hate you, Tair," she roared at the ceiling as the pillow came down at her. She caught it neatly and tossed it again. "I will hate you forever!"

Damn him.

They shouldn't have ever had fun together. Much less really good sex. One could forget a man that was bad company, a man that was rude, crude, boorish. But sexy? Mysterious? Powerful? Interesting? Tender?

Stop thinking about him, she told herself. Stop thinking about the desert, and the starlit nights. Stop thinking about his smelly goatskin tents and the acrid smell of smoke and the fire burning late into the night. Put all thoughts of soft silk pillows and handwoven rugs and the perfume of roses and orange blossoms out of mind. Pretend you never slept curved against Tair's side, his arm around you, your cheek against his chest. Pretend you never listened to his heartbeat. Pretend you don't know every scar on his face and torso. Pretend you didn't lie awake some nights and worry about him, worry about his foolish courage, his lack of fear, his inability to protect himself as long as someone else is in danger…

Tally caught the pillow again and clutched it to her chest.

He'd never put himself first, not when others are in danger.

As she'd been in danger.

Tally felt the prickle start inside her, in her chest, and then her throat, working from the inside out until her forehead had the same tingling and her heart beat faster, harder, beat with a strange sense of awareness, an awareness that hadn't been there until a moment ago. But now that the thought was there it wasn't going away…

And she didn't know what to think.

Could Tair have sent her away, not because he didn't love her, but because he did?

Goose bumps covered her arms, the fine little hairs standing and everything inside her seemed to be turning inward, listening. Listening to her heart.

Listening to instinct, because wasn't that what Tair had taught her? Not to listen to the voice of fear, but the voice of calm inside her? The voice of strength?

He didn't not care for her.

He did.

He did.

She jumped up from the sofa, crossed the floor in long jerky strides, arms folded over her chest and tears hot and cold burned her eyes.

It hit her. Hit her so hard. Tair sent her away because he didn't want her hurt. He sent her away because he was afraid he couldn't protect her. He sent her away because he couldn't bear to have her hurt.

My God.

Why hadn't she seen it before? Understood?

Tally stopped at the loft window overlooking the street. It was a Sunday afternoon and traffic was light. No football game at the Seahawks stadium, no crowds, summer tourists gone. Just late afternoon sun breaking through the bank of clouds, splinters of long gold light and the green and yellow trolley traveling between all-brick buildings.

Here she was, safe in Seattle, just the way Tair wanted. But how was he? Where was he? What was he doing?

Tally stood at the window a long time, long enough to watch the clouds clear and the sun set, and the gold and red colors of autumn give way to burnt-orange and purple of dusk.

When it was dark, the sun gone, sunlight replaced by street lamps, Tally knew what she had to do. Knew where she had to go. Knew it wouldn't be easy but she was Tair's woman and she had to be where he was. It wasn't an option. She had no choice.

Two long flights, one terrifying helicopter landing, and a camel ride later, Tally had to admit that things were going badly.

She'd only been back in Ouaha twenty-four hours and she'd already been robbed, and left for dead. Not an auspicious return. Not exactly the homecoming she'd envisioned. She'd imagined well…not this.

And this was sand. Just lots and lots of sand. And this time Tair didn't even know she was back. Tair didn't know she'd decided to return. There'd be no daring rescue now.

Tally exhaled, and pulled a strand of hair from her eyelashes and tried to get more comfortable on her shirt which was protecting her from the burning grains of sand.

This was not the place to be.

She was parched, so thirsty she'd begun to see mirages in the sand. Dancing girls. Swaying palm trees. Robed warriors with swords and whips.·

And guns. Or more accurately, one gun.

Tally blinked, looked up against the dazzling sun, head aching from the heat. A man stood in front of her, armed, fierce. Hideous. She frowned irritably, lifting a hand to block the sun and erase the mirage. "If you're not real, go away."

She heard a sigh, a very long drawn-out exasperated sigh. The kind of sigh only a man who is very long-suffering can make. "I'm real, and I'm not going away."

Tally tried to leap up but she wobbled and nearly fell, courtesy dehydration and a nasty case of sunstroke.

With a muttered oath, Tair lifted her in his arms, dropped her on his horse and climbed into the saddle behind her. They rode for an hour or more—Tally couldn't tell, didn't even really care—and then they arrived to the most pitiful desert camp Tally had ever seen.

"This place is still pathetic," she said as Tair swung her out of the saddle and onto the ground.

"We didn't have time to pick flowers or hang new gingham curtains," Tair said, circling Tally's wrist with his hand and pulling her after him.

Tally spotted Tair's old Berber servant and went to lift a hand in friendly greeting. Tair shot her a hard look. "Don't," he snapped. "I'm not in the mood."

Once in his tent, with Tally sitting on cushions on the carpeted floor Tair demanded an answer. Only he didn't put it quite that nicely. His request came out more like, "What the hell are you doing here?"

She could be offended. She ought to be offended. But she knew Tair better. "I brought you something," she said, reaching into her bra and pulling out the warm and very extravagant necklace.

Tair took the glittering emerald and diamond necklace from her. "You came all this way to return jewelry?"

"Yes."

"What's wrong with the postal service?"

Outside Tair's tent the men had begun to lay the fire for dinner and the little three-legged dog came hopping along. Tally looked at the licks of red and gold flames, the flea-bitten dog and Tair's dark, fierce scowling face.

"I wanted to be sure it'd reach you," she answered.

He made a rough inarticulate sound. "I take it you're not fond of emeralds?"

"It's a beautiful necklace but I'm not going to accept a gift like that. It's absurd. You send me away—reject me, break my heart—and then give me a necklace worth a quarter of a million dollars?"

The corner of his mouth curved. "How do you know its value?"

"I had it appraised." She stared him down. "And no, courier companies won't accept a $250,000 necklace, not if the address happens to be in the middle of the Sahara."

She snorted. "Can you imagine me trying to give directions? Tell your driver it's four hours east of El Saroush by horseback, or six if traveling by camel. Somewhere you'll encounter a riverbed and then you take a left at the wadi. Another hour later, you'll pass a cluster of palm trees. That's where you take a right. And then sometime in the next hour—or hour and a half depending on how fast you're traveling—you'll veer north and hope to find the rock fortress."

He smiled. "Your distances are off but the landmarks are good."

She hardened herself to his wretched barbarian charm. His smile wouldn't work on her this time, nor his offhand compliment. She knew him too well. Knew exactly how he operated. Bluster, power, intimidation, and sex appeal. A deadly combination if she'd ever heard one.

"The point is, *Tair*, you can't send *ex-wives* gifts like that and not expect them to fly off the handle."

"You do seem angry."

"I'm furious."

"But you're always furious."

"Because you're always trying to pull a fast one on me!"

"And how did I do that this time?"

"The necklace. You're trying to buy me. You were using emeralds to ease your guilt. You send me a necklace, tell me to have a good life, and you think I'm going to go—ooh! A lovely necklace. That's wonderful. My husband doesn't want me, and he won't love me, but he's sent me some really pretty jewels!"

Tair shifted on his haunches. "Are you telling me it didn't work?"

"I'm telling you—" She broke off, stared at him, shook her head in disbelief. "You're such a liar and manipulator and—" Tally didn't even try to finish the sentence. Instead she crept forward, clasped Tair's face in her hands and kissed him deeply.

It was a long time before she ended the kiss. His mouth on hers was too electric and she'd missed him too much. But finally she had to get some control, finish making her point, and reluctantly she sat back to study him again. "You love me."

"I don't."

"You do." She hesitated, hating the whispers of insecurity. *"Tair."*

"What?" he asked innocently.

But before she could answer he reached out and gently

plucked a hair from her eyes, and then another from her cheek. He smoothed the thick strands back from her face, his hand infinitely gentle as he touched her. "I do."

Tally sat very still, the air bottled in her lungs. She couldn't look away from his dark eyes and hard jaw and the strange expression on his face. It was torment. Agony. "What's wrong?"

"Everything."

"But I'm here, Tair."

"Yes, I know, and I can't handle it, Tally. I can't bear it if anything should happen to you. I can lose my arms, my legs, my life—but I can't lose you."

"You won't."

"I could."

"Tair, I'm stronger than I look. I haven't had an asthma attack since the day we met."

His jaw gentled. He nearly smiled but then the darkness returned to his eyes and his pain was there, in his face. "I'm afraid for you. Afraid for you every single day you're here."

"I don't understand, Tair—"

"Ara died here. My wife—and my son. I held Zaki as he died, I held him and couldn't save him, and I can't do that again. I can't. It would kill me and where would my people be?"

"Tair."

"I thought I could protect you, Tally, but when you were taken from the garden, when they held you hostage I couldn't do anything for you—"

"But you did, you found me, you rescued me."

He shook his head. His dark eyes were shadowed with pain and suffering. "I was sure there'd be blood. I could see it all happening, what they could do to you. I was sure I would be too late." His jaw tensed and he swallowed even as he reached out to lightly trace the curve of her cheekbone and then her upper lip that bowed. "You are too beautiful, Tally.

I would rather live far from you and know you live, than have you here and know you suffer."

"But I suffer when I'm away from you, Tair."

His eyes narrowed. A small muscle pulled in his cheek. "Death is worse."

"But away from you is death, too."

He turned his head, looked away, thick black lashes fringing his eyes, concealing the sheen of tears. "It isn't right to risk so much. It is selfish of me—"

"It's selfish of you to send me away when I love you and want to be with you. It's selfish of you to tell me I must be a coward and afraid. It's not my nature to be fearful. It's my nature to risk, and to want change."

"Tally." His voice broke.

"Tair, don't fear for me. And don't make decisions for me. I know the risks. I know what's at stake but I'd rather have a month with you than a lifetime without."

He reached up to shove hair back from his face. "That's ridiculous," he answered gruffly.

She leaned forward and reached out to catch the single tear on his lashes and wipe it away. "But romantic."

"And foolish."

"And exciting."

"You'll be the death of me," he muttered, even as he turned to her and lifted her face between his hands. He studied her face for an endless moment, his dark gaze searching her eyes, searching for truth, searching for the answer that seemed to elude him.

"I like exciting, Tair," she whispered.

The corner of his mouth reluctantly tugged. "You're impossible."

"But you like that, too."

He bent his head, touched his mouth to her forehead and then her cheekbone and finally her mouth. "You're beautiful."

His smile wasn't entirely steady. "You're exactly perfect, Tally."

"You called me Tally."

"I know. What was I thinking?"

She scooted toward him, practically climbing into his lap. "I don't know. But just keep me, Tair. That's all I ask. Keep me close to you."

"I thought you were a wandering woman. Someone who couldn't stay in one place long."

She blinked hard, blinked to keep the tears from falling. He undid her. He, barbarian that he was, made her heart hurt and hope in ways she'd never thought possible. "That was before I met you."

"You're a changed woman, are you?"

"Mmmmm."

"What's that?"

She tried to avoid his searching gaze but he wasn't letting her evade him. Tally sighed exasperatedly. "Maybe not that changed."

"So why can you stay here with me?"

"Because you're the ultimate challenge. You're Mount Everest and the Amazon put together. How could I tire of you? I'll never completely understand you but—" She broke off, took a quick, deep breath. "But I promise I'll always try."

Creases fanned from his eyes. His fierce features were inexplicably gentle, and the warmth in his eyes tangible. He stroked her cheekbone, and then the curve of her mouth, her soft pouting upper lip, the full lower lip and then down to her chin. "I love you. And I need you. I'm lost—" He broke off, struggled with the words, then forced himself to finish. "Without you. Come home."

She moved the rest of the way into his arms. "I have."

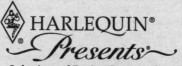

HARLEQUIN *Presents*

Coming Next Month

#2547 PRINCE OF THE DESERT Penny Jordan
Arabian Nights

Gwynneth had vowed that she would never become a slave to passion. But one hot night of lovemaking with a stranger from the desert has left her fevered and unsure. Little does Gwynneth know that she shared a bed with Sheikh Tariq bin Salud.

#2548 THE SCORSOLINI MARRIAGE BARGAIN Lucy Monroe
Royal Brides

Claudio Scorsolini married Therese for convenience only. So when Therese starts to fall in love with her husband, she tries to end the marriage—for both their sakes. But Claudio isn't ready to let her go.

#2549 NAKED IN HIS ARMS Sandra Marton
UnCut

When ex-Special Forces agent Alexander Knight is called upon to protect the beautiful Cara Prescott, his only choice is to hide her on his private island. But can Alex keep Cara from harm when he has no idea how dangerous the truth really is?

#2550 THE SECRET BABY REVENGE Emma Darcy
Latin Lovers

Joaquin Luis Sola is proud and passionate and yearns to possess beautiful Nicole Ashton. Nicole reluctantly offers herself to him, if he will pay her debts. This proposition promises that Quin will see a most satisfying return.

#2551 AT THE GREEK TYCOON'S BIDDING Cathy Williams
Greek Tycoons

Heather is different from Greek businessman Theo Miquel's usual prey: frumpy, far too talkative and his office cleaner. But Theo could see she would be perfect for an affair—at his beck and call until he tires of her. But Heather won't stay at her boss's bidding!

#2552 THE ITALIAN'S CONVENIENT WIFE Catherine Spencer
Italian Husbands

When Paolo Rainero's niece and nephew are orphaned, his solution is to marry Caroline Leighton, their American aunt, with whom Paolo once had a fling. Their desire is rekindled from years before—but Caroline has a secret....

#2553 THE JET-SET SEDUCTION Sandra Field
Foreign Affairs

From the moment Slade Carruthers lays eyes on Clea Chardin he knows he must have her. But Clea has a reputation, and Slade isn't a man to share his spoils. If Clea wants to come to his bed, she will come on his terms.

#2554 MISTRESS ON DEMAND Maggie Cox
Mistress to a Millionaire

Rich and irresistible, property tycoon Dominic van Straten lived in an entirely different world from Sophie's. But after their reckless hot encounter, Dominic wanted her available whenever he needed her.